In memory of
many happy times
in Spain

Burton Graham
(Bill to you)

THE SPY TRAP

The Spy Trap

BURTON GRAHAM

LONDON

J. M. DENT & SONS LTD

First published 1971

Made in Great Britain
at the
Aldine Press · Letchworth · Herts
for
J. M. DENT & SONS LTD
Aldine House · Bedford Street · London

ISBN 0 460 03987 3

I

The snow-covered mountains and valleys of Central Austria slid by in the darkness and the train glided through the night towards Vienna. Evans looked at his watch and wondered if the mission had been completed—if Hannifin had dead-dropped the Eisendrath documents to Pravja and was already waiting at the airport. Eleven-thirty. It could be all over by now. And by three o'clock he and Hannifin would be on the plane bound for London. Mission accomplished.

Evans sat back and listened to the pleasant tattoo of the wheels and the whirring rush of the express through the cold dark night. It was warm and comfortable in the carriage. But he couldn't relax. Too much was at stake tonight. Not only the work of ten months, but a result that could have a bearing on the future of Czechoslovakia. And something more. It was Hannifin's first mission.

Hannifin. Evans grinned when he thought of the struggle he'd had to get him. C had wanted to foist Towery on him. What C hadn't understood was that this was a different type of operation and that the situation had called for an unorthodox approach, a new breed of operative. Well, Hannifin had certainly justified his choice.

In fact—and he had to admit it—during the past few weeks he'd felt slightly redundant. Hannifin was the only contact with Eisendrath. Hannifin was the producer, the one who'd got the goods and dead-dropped them to Pravja, the Czech. He, Evans, had been the decoy, the dried pea in the old-style sleight-of-hand game he'd put on to confuse Grubenko and finally to lure him away from Vienna while Hannifin made the kill.

The train rocketed into a tunnel. Evans tapped his pipe on his shoe and settled more comfortably in the corner of the carriage. Maybe Hannifin was the shape of things to come. Maybe even spring was having to adapt itself to the new world of youth, a world Evans didn't particularly like. Maybe the experienced careful old-timer like himself, or the rather sleazy nondescript cloak-and-dagger sleuth like Towery, was obsolescent. Maybe the battle of the future would be fought on the intellectual level of Hannifin. The thought made Evans feel older than his forty-one years. Here he was, thinking of Tim Hannifin almost as though he were his son.

The train whooshed out of the tunnel and a little later entered the last leg of the journey.

Evans roused himself when the train gave a long whistle and its galloping tattoo began to change. The speed slackened and he saw buildings and sidings gliding by. Lights shone brightly on the rails beside the train. The bright lights of Vienna.

The train slid quietly to a halt.

As soon as Evans cleared the vast platform area he sought a telephone booth and dialled a number.

'Hallo.' It was Pravja's deep, intense voice.

Evans said: 'This is Anstruther. I am ringing to inquire if my package has arrived.'

'No.' The Czech's voice sounded terse, bad-tempered.

'Thank you. I shall ring again in an hour.'

'Very well.'

The line went dead.

Evans hung up and stepped out of the booth. He was stunned and slightly rattled. Pravja's reply had told him that Hannifin had made no contact since going to dine with Eisendrath. He checked his watch. It was just after one o'clock. Something must have gone wrong.

In a fine drizzle of rain he took a cab to his hotel and located his second drive-yourself car in the parking area. He got in and drove to the secondary rendezvous point where Pravja was waiting. Maybe Hannifin had rung in.

Evans had been loaned to the Czech underground to help protect it from a Soviet-directed counter-espionage organization operating throughout Austria and East Germany. MI5 had become convinced that Vienna was its headquarters and that Kolya Grubenko, the Russian KGB operative, had set it up, using hard-core Communists and members of the so-called intelligentsia. Evans had come to Vienna ten months ago as a British machine-tool salesman and had trailed Grubenko. This had led him to Doctor Eisendrath, a senior lecturer at the University of Vienna. As time went on, other leads had led to Eisendrath, and Evans had become convinced that the doctor of philosophy was a key figure.

Evans realized that he would have to get someone close to Eisendrath. He went back to London for assistance. C gave him the choice of four experienced SIS men, including Towery, one of the best. But Evans had a plan that called for a different type. He'd had Hannifin in mind from the start: Hannifin, a brilliant young teacher at the London School of Economics. For a time, C insisted on Towery, but finally gave way to Evans's stubborn demands. Evans was given the green light. He approached Hannifin, recruited him, trained him, then brought him to Vienna. C was able to fix up a special scholarship which sent Hannifin to the University of Vienna for special studies in philosophy.

The plan had worked well. Doctor Eisendrath had taken an instant interest in Hannifin and had invited him to his home a number of times for philosophical discussions. At these meetings, held in the doctor's library, Hannifin had kept his eyes and ears open. On one occasion when Eisendrath was called to the phone he made a brief search of the doctor's desk and found a significant document, which he photographed. From then on, after each meeting Hannifin would drive to the canal-end of Petersplatz and dead-drop an account of the meeting to Pravja, a member of the Czech underground attached to Evans.

A week ago, Evans decided the time was ripe to act. He instructed Hannifin to gain a further invitation to Eisendrath's home. During coffee and liqueurs after dinner in his host's library, Hannifin was to drug him, search his desk and safe, dead-drop the information to Pravja and fly back to London. Evans, having checked with Pravja that the mission had been accomplished, would fly back with him and report to C.

All went according to plan. On Wednesday, Hannifin reported that he had received an invitation to dine with Eisendrath on the following Sunday evening. Evans made a move to get Grubenko and his watch-dogs out of the way. He questioned the *concierge* of the apartment block where Grubenko was staying, then parked opposite and watched the building. After a time he drove back to his hotel. Late that night he packed an overnight bag, took it down to the parking area and made a deliberate show of checking the motor and tyres of one of his two drive-yourself hire cars. He drove out of Vienna and all the way to Deggendorf, a town not far south of the Czech border. Grubenko took the bait and followed with three of his hatchet-men.

For two days Evans hung round the town, sent off a number of ambiguous telegrams, including one to the public library in Prague, and generally acted like a spy trying not to act like a spy. He succeeded in selling the idea to Grubenko that he was a British agent waiting for a meeting with the leaders of the Czech underground. In the early hours of Sunday morning Evans left his car parked outside the hotel and cut out of town by jumping a goods train. Certain that no one had followed him, at Munich he caught a passenger train to Vienna.

But something had gone wrong.

Hannifin hadn't shown up in Petersplatz to dead-drop the information at the appointed time, and Pravja was still at the *pension*. As Evans drove there now he prepared himself for the possibility that Hannifin might never again be seen alive.

8

The Czech lit a cigarette and refilled his glass with cognac. Then he sat on the bed.

'I waited for an hour!' he snapped. He was shivering. His wet topcoat was slung over a chair.

Evans said: 'And he didn't show up?'

'That is right!' Pravja looked up at him, resenting the question and Evans's whole manner. He said shortly: 'I was two minutes early. That is the rule!'

'Let me see your watch.'

Pravja stuck out a hairy wrist and looked insolently at the picture on the wall, an amateurish oil-painting of the Danube. Evans examined the dial of the watch and checked it with his own. For a moment he looked down at the Czech's young, bad-tempered face. It appeared sallow and ugly in the half-light and his dark, intelligent eyes glinted with defiance under the shock of bristling black hair.

Evans turned away and picked up the drink Pravja had poured for him. It was harsh and difficult to get down. He was still wearing his brown felt hat and British gabardine overcoat. He was ten years older than the Czech, but looked more. He was about medium height, Welsh, good-looking in a tough, roguish way, with a fighter's beetle brows and a slightly crooked nose. He turned toward the window and said:

'Douse the light.'

The Czech twisted round quickly, cigarette between his lips, and switched off the bedside lamp. The room was plunged into darkness.

Evans parted the curtains and looked into the street. There was no traffic, and though it was after one-thirty the street lights were still on. There was a white halo around each mist-dimmed light. The street was shining with moisture. The only vehicles he could see were his own and Pravja's.

Evans's voice cut through the blackness inside the room: 'You are certain there's no misunderstanding?'

'How could there be?'

'He contacted you by phone?'

'Yes.'

'What time?'

'Just after six. He sounded the same as usual.'

'How was that?'

'Businesslike. Kind of terse.'

Evans was silent. He was clutching at straws. He asked more calmly: 'What did Hannifin say? Give it to me word for word.'

Pravja hesitated. His voice sounded selfconscious in the darkness. 'It was Hannifin's voice. I'm certain of that. He said: "Herr Reimer, I am ringing to say I will be late. I have to meet my sister at the Sudbahnhof at eleven-fifty."' He explained needlessly: 'Which meant a dead-drop at the canal-end of Petersplatz at 23.50 hours.'

There was a long silence. The mist looked dense. It was not a fog but a gentle mist of fine soaking rain. A young man came striding along the pavement. He wore a cloth cap and his hands were in the pockets of his short topcoat. He was whistling softly to himself. A lover going home to his own bed. His ears must be wet.

Evans groped for the answer. The drop had been arranged for 23.50—more than an hour and a half ago. Hannifin hadn't turned up in Petersplatz, and he still hadn't checked in by phone. The vital information he'd stolen from Doctor Eisendrath this evening was still in his possession. Evans stared at the black silhouette of the university buildings, dimly visible through the darkness. Beyond them he saw in his mind the great rococo buildings and the ghostly city of Vienna. Somewhere out there, somewhere in this city, in the darkness, was Tim Hannifin, with the Eisendrath dossier still in his possession. He closed the curtains, crossed in the darkness and switched on the lamp.

The Czech looked at his watch and stood up, his glass half empty. There was no heating in the room and he wanted to go. He stood and rocked on his heels a little selfconsciously and swirled the brandy in his glass. Evans looked at him and could tell he was uncomfortable about something and wanted to get out of the *pension*.

Evans asked: 'What do *you* think has gone wrong?'

'I don't know.'

'But there's something on your mind.'

Pravja looked again at the painting. 'There is nothing.'

'Yes, there is, Jan! And I want to know what it is!'

The Czech's mouth was drawn down at the corners. He said nothing.

Evans said: 'You have your own idea where Hannifin is, haven't you?'

'He might be with a girl—the girl he's been sleeping with.'

The words were spoken quietly, falling on the silence in the cold, threadbare *pension*. Pravja turned his eyes to meet Evans's. He'd hated himself for his squirming evasions.

Evans had hated him too. And if this was the truth, bitter as it was, it was better than knowing nothing. 'What girl?' he asked softly.

'She lives at the Kaiserhof.'

'How long has he been sleeping with her?'

'Three nights—since you went to Deggendorf.'

'How do you *know* this?'

'I have to look after my own skin.'

'How do you *know*?' Evans persisted.

Pravja said evenly: 'Another Czech. I used to know him in Plzen. He works at the Kaiserhof as a waiter——'

Evans cut in accusingly: 'You've been spying on Hannifin!'

'I have to—to protect myself—and the underground.'

'You've been spying on him!'

'Yes.' Pravja sat on the bed and folded his arms. He said bluntly: 'Working with Hannifin is not like working with you, Mike! There is something missing with Hannifin!'

Evans stood over him, waiting for an explanation. He was livid.

Pravja flung out: 'I could smell a woman on him!'

'So?'

'So I had to look into it! I felt unsafe! I felt I couldn't trust him any longer!'

Evans turned away. He didn't want to hear any more. Not until Hannifin was here. He wanted Hannifin to come through that door and prove the Czech wrong. He said: 'Who is the woman?'

The bitter tone of Evans's voice jolted Pravja. 'She's no whore, Mike! She's a nice girl——'

'Who is she?'

'She's a correspondent for an American press syndicate.'

'Sara Collins?'

'Yes.'

Evans felt immediate relief. He put his cold pipe into his mouth and bit on the stem. Sara Collins. He'd met her twice recently with a CIA man in Vienna. His mind gave him a momentary vision of a small-boned girl with a large mouth and wide dark brown eyes behind outlandishly large horn-rimmed spectacles that made her look like Betty Boop. She worked for United Press and was usually based in West Berlin. She was in Vienna to cover the opening of tomorrow's peace conference, one of a series leading to the Summit.

He was furious with Hannifin. Furious with him for committing the one unpardonable sin a spy could commit. He had lost his head. He'd jeopardized months of work at the most critical stage of the operation and had compromised Evans and the whole Czech underground. Evans had drummed this into Hannifin right from the start—as C had done to all the MI5 field men. Never—never—lose your head—over a woman, money, fear, panic, or for any other reason.

He turned abruptly and picked up the telephone directory from the bedside table and quickly thumbed through the leaves. He found the number of the Kaiserhof and picked up the phone and dialled. The night clerk answered and Evans asked for Fräulein Collins's room.

He heard the ring and the change in dial-tone. Almost at

once a low voice came on the line, soft, slightly breathless.

'Yes?'

'Sara Collins?'

'Yes.'

'It's Mike Evans.'

He heard the sudden intake of breath. 'Mike!'

'Is Tim Hannifin with you?'

'No!'

'Where is he?'

'I don't know! I thought he was with you! He told me you were both flying out to London tonight!'

'He told *you* that?'

'He trusts me. He told me everything.'

'Christ! When did you last see him?'

'At five o'clock.'

'He's been with you all day?'

'Yes.'

'And all last night?'

'Yes.'

'And the night before that?'

'Yes.'

'I see.'

'What's the matter? Has something gone wrong?'

'I'll tell you in the morning after I've found him!' He was about to hang up.

'Mike!' Her voice sounded urgent, pleading.

'Yes?'

'Mike. I—I love him. He says he's going to get a divorce. Do you think that's true?'

Evans hesitated. 'If he said so, it probably is.'

'Thanks.'

He hung up.

He picked up the glass of cognac and drank half of it. Then he put it down and said: 'Christ! A bloody newspaper woman! He told her everything!' He didn't know what to say to Pravja.

13

The Czech had made his point and felt sorry about it. He wanted to go. He rose and said: 'Look, Mike. I'm cold and wet. And I can't do anything more tonight. I want to go back to my place.'

Evans said tersely: 'Hannifin will ring on this number!'

'But he knows *my* number too!'

'He wouldn't use it. It would put you in too much danger!'

Pravja stood uncertainly. He had no faith in anything Hannifin might do.

Evans said bluntly: 'Sit down and have another cognac and sweat it out! You've got to wait for his telephone call! Don't you understand? Hannifin's on the run! Either that or he's made a botch of it and he's dead!'

He stuffed his pipe back in his pocket and began to pull on his fur-lined gloves.

'Where are you going?' Pravja asked.

'Out to look for him.'

The Czech was pouring himself another drink. 'Do you think that is wise?'

Evans ignored him. He let himself out and stole quietly along the corridor. He walked down two flights of stairs to the dimly lit hallway, went past the *concierge*'s room, opened the front door and stepped out into the street. He crossed the pavement to the parked Renault and opened the door.

A black figure had emerged from the shadows of the stairway leading to the basement. It reached the cobbled pavement and moved quickly and silently behind him. Evans heard the soft *pad* of a leather sole and whirled. He saw a man with a black stocking pulled over his face, and the flash of a blade, low down. An icicle-sharp stiletto drove through his top-coat, through his coat, his shirt, his singlet, broke the skin an inch below his left ribs and plunged through to his back and was pulled out, dripping red. Evans uttered a strangled gurgling groan as he sagged and fell to the ground. He heard footsteps pelting across the cobbled road and saw mountains rushing by as he slid into a long black tunnel.

2

He woke up in a bed in a clean white room. He learned later that Pravja had seen the attack from the window of the *pension*, had rung for an ambulance and had him rushed to the nearby University Hospital. He didn't know much about what happened during the next week as he lingered between life and death. He drifted in and out of consciousness a number of times. Sometimes there would be a doctor standing by the bedside saying something to him. At other times it would be in the dead of night and a nurse with a white oval face would administer a bottle and give him a sedative and he would go back to sleep. Then it would be day and another nurse—a prettier one with slightly buck teeth—would spoon-feed him some baby food. Nearly every time he awoke, he was told later, he would ask for Hannifin. Speaking was painful, but he would attempt to say: 'Hannifin!' 'Where's Hannifin?' 'Get Hannifin!' Once he woke to find Sara Collins there. She was sitting on a chair beside the bed. The pretty nurse was standing by the foot of the bed. Sara's face looked pale and wan.

'Hallo, Mike,' she said.

She rose and leaned over him and held her cheek next to his. Her skin felt cool against his and he knew he must have a stubble. He didn't know how long it was since he'd shaved. She straightened and stood close to the bed looking down at him.

She blinked several times and said: 'Tim has disappeared.'

He lay there looking up into her face. She didn't have her glasses on today. He guessed she was wearing her contacts. Her small slightly pug nose had freckles on it. He wondered if the Viennese nurse thought she was his daughter.

'You hate me, don't you?'

He stared up at her and thought of Hannifin's stupidity and wondered where he was.

She said: 'You blame me for Tim's fouling up.'

She stood looking at him helplessly. Her eyes were moist, blinking. After a time she went out of focus and faded off.

There was sunlight in the room. It must have been late afternoon. Towery was there. The sunlight threw his distorted profile onto the white wall. He was sitting beside the bed. You couldn't tell how long he'd been there. Towery was like that— like a scrawny ginger cat watching a mousehole.

He said: 'Hallo, Mike.'

'Hallo.'

'How are you feeling?'

'Where's Hannifin?'

Towery hesitated. 'He's not here.'

'Where is he?'

'Hannifin's defected. He's in Moscow.'

The bitter details came out as Towery plodded round Vienna sniffing out the meagre clues. Pravja helped him, of course, and the more Towery found out the worse it made Evans look.

Towery, with his years of experience and his unblemished record. Towery, seedy, hard-drinking, callous. There was a streak of personal vanity in Towery that frightened Evans.

Towery was here in Vienna to prove a point, and to rub Evans's nose in the dirt if he could. He got his opportunity, for it soon became evident that Hannifin had been working as a double agent for weeks. Pravja had been suspicious of him for over a fortnight. The truth came out now that Hannifin had alerted the whole anti-underground network. Only

Pravja's timely warning to the underground had saved it from annihilation. Having rung Pravja at the arranged time on Sunday evening, Hannifin had caught a taxi to the airport and boarded a plane for Warsaw. While Pravja was getting drenched at the canal-end of Petersplatz waiting for the dead-drop that would never come, Hannifin was sitting back in the comfort of a pressurized cabin. He was now in Moscow with Philby and Burgess and Maclean and . . . Oh, Christ . . .

Evans heard it all in silence as Towery told it to him before catching a plane back to London to make his report to C. And for a long time after, Mike stared at the flowers Sara had brought him. They reminded him of a meadow near Kahlenberg. He'd gone there one Sunday morning. The sun was bright and warm. He stood among the flowers and shrubs and trees. The whole scene was alive with butterflies and birds. But now he knew it was not like that at all. Everything in space was night and silence, a vast dark hall seeking its way in gloom. Life was only a momentary pinpoint of light. He slept for several hours.

When he awoke it was evening. The pretty nurse brought him a full three-course meal. He was hungry and enjoyed it. He was just cleaning up the last of the apple fritters when Sara Collins came in. She was wearing her Betty Boops.

The moment he saw her he knew that something had happened. Her eyes had a funny look in them. A funny hurt look that said: I don't understand. I bruise easily and I've been hurt. But I don't understand.

She said: 'I've heard from Tim.'

Evans didn't say anything. She waited until an orderly had cleared the dishes away and gone out.

'He's asked me to join him in Moscow.'

'Christ Almighty.'

She was going to say something but stopped herself. She opened her handbag and took a bulky envelope from it, slipped out several pages folded together and smoothed them out on her knee. She began to read.

Evans listened dully to Hannifin's confession. It made sour reading. Hannifin's recent actions were no aberration. From the letter it soon became plain that they were only the climax to a carefully thought out plan. He had got himself into the Secret Service with exactly this in mind—no doubt influenced by Kim Philby. Evans always thought he'd recruited Hannifin, contrived to meet him a number of times, subtly cultivated him, gradually caught his interest and finally his dedication, then recruited him to the Service with the backing of his own reputation, his own record. It was not so, apparently. As he listened, it seemed certain that Hannifin had played him like a plump eager trout.

Sara went on reading: '"There's a lot wrong with the Soviet regime. I do not agree with the persecution of Soviet writers, or in the present policy of stifling every anti-Party thought in the country, but this does not alter what Communism *is*. Mistakes of policy and the evil done by some leaders can have no effect on my faith."'

She paused and looked at him. Evans nodded. At least it was an honest confession, though it seemed too pat. The whole thing seemed too pat, as though Philby—or Eisendrath—had been advising him from the start. But there was something wrong, even with that.

'"You will have heard by this about my defection. I want you to know that our time in Vienna was not part of any plan. It was meant to be a passing affair. I didn't intend to fall in love with you. As a matter of fact, on that final Sunday I did some pretty solid soul-searching and even thought I might be wrong, that I should give up my mission and marry you and Capitalism."'

Evans said: 'Collins and Capitalism. The supreme sacrifice.'

'"But then I knew I couldn't do this. I decided instead to defect first and ask you to marry me afterwards. Then the choice would be yours."' She folded the letter and said: 'And he asks me to go to Moscow and marry him. He says he can get an immediate divorce.'

Evans nodded. 'KGB people are favoured.'

He watched her as she slipped the letter into its envelope and put it back in her handbag. He felt sorry for her, even sorrier than he felt for himself.

She looked down at him steadily. Her eyes blinked a few times. 'You don't have to worry about me. I have printer's ink in my veins. And something occurred to me about *that* too.'

'What's that?'

'I'm a journalist. I write for a powerful syndicate. Tim would know that when he met me.'

Evans nodded. 'I've thought of that.'

'Do you think he may have wooed me because of my syndicate?'

'Well, you're much prettier than Ursula Funger of AAP.'

'And my readership's greater.' She suddenly took the envelope from her handbag and waved it in front of his nose. 'This letter would make good copy. A beautiful scoop for Sara Collins!' She put it back and said: 'All right, Tim Hannifin. I'll write it! But not the way you want it!' She said: 'I'll write it tonight. But I shan't scoop it. I'll write it and hold it.'

He looked up at her. The little freckle-nosed reporter from Nebraska or somewhere. It seemed funny to him that she was an important pawn in such a big game.

She said: 'The knife attack in the dead of night on the man who was his friend and mentor. Hannifin was no lofty idealist fighting for a better world. His tactics were those of any back-alley thug! Will you help me write it, Mike?'

He looked at her for a long time. Then he nodded vaguely. 'Why not?'

After she'd gone, he thought about Hannifin and his letter. It was too pat, too smug, like a well-turned-out radio script. It didn't sit. He remembered Hannifin reporting with relish his first step with Eisendrath. It happened during a lecture on the Purpose of Philosophy in the Twentieth Century. Hannifin put forward a rather groping, slightly inarticulate suggestion that he thought philosophy's real task today was, somehow, to produce realities and, somehow, to determine the nature of the world of tomorrow. Eisendrath had bitten on the bait. He invited Hannifin to dinner at his home the following Sunday evening.

This was the opening gambit in an intellectual chase-me-catch-me. The stake, in Hannifin's mind, was to get close to Eisendrath for Evans's purposes. Evans thought now that the stake in Eisendrath's mind was Hannifin himself. Tim reported how the doctor had led him gradually toward the concept of 'total planning without recognition of limits'. Evans recognized it as Marxism, but had felt Hannifin was safe. But he'd been wrong. And something impinged, something to do with Hannifin's letter. It worried Evans until he dozed off.

Sara kept coming to see him. She brought him flowers, several books, blocks of chocolate and a bottle of Scotch. In fact, she was as loving and attentive as a wife. Mike thought it was because he was her only link with Tim. Or maybe that she blamed herself for what had happened to him. It worried him slightly because he'd steered clear of involvements since the break-up of his marriage—not that he thought for a moment he was getting involved with Sara. But everything about marriage had annoyed him. Relationships he didn't want, arguments he didn't want and couldn't cope with, time and money-wasting activities that led nowhere. Once was enough. He knew he was a loner, a solitary. He liked it that way.

One evening he told her he was leaving. 'I fly out to London tomorrow. So I guess this is "goodbye".'

Her face clouded. 'But, Mike! You're not well enough!'

'Nonsense. I should have gone a week ago.'

'But what will you do when you get to London?'

'Convalesce.'

'You'd be better convalescing here, or in Spain!'

'I'll be all right.'

'Where will you be?'

'In my flat in Chelsea.'

She took his hand impulsively. 'Let me come and take care of you!'

He shook his head.

'Please.'

'What about your job?'

'I'll take a month off.'

'No.'

'Please.'

He shook his head.

Vienna Airport slid away below, and to Mike Evans it was watching part of his life sliding away and being left behind, an untidy, unsatisfactory part that had ended abruptly in an inglorious and costly debacle. He knew that something very bitter lay ahead. For it could be read clearly in Towery's report that Evans had rendered the SIS a disservice and that as a consequence there would be foreseeable and unforeseeable repercussions. Hannifin, now in the enemy camp, knew a great deal about the SIS. Evans found himself going back over his time with Hannifin, trying to gauge the value of everything he'd told him initially as a recruit and later as an agent working closely with him.

Evans knew he'd given Hannifin all the background of MI5's most notable failures. Burgess, Maclean, the Philby calamity, the mysterious disappearance of Commander Crabb. He'd impressed on Hannifin the fact that such calamities rendered irreparable harm and greatly affected the morale and stature of a country's security services and compromised it in its relations with its allies and with other nations. This was why the defection of an SIS man and the resultant world-wide publicity were so disastrous and far-reaching. And he knew that Hannifin's defection would be no exception.

Some time later the plane began its descent. The grey waters of the Channel were not far below.

3

A week went by and nothing happened. No one called. No one from the Department telephoned. Apparently it was not good strategy to be friendly with an agent whose recruit had defected.

There was only one man Evans wanted to talk to. Only one man mattered. This was C himself. And Evans found himself *wanting* the summons, *wanting* to talk it out with C. Control, head of the SIS, was the very antithesis of the bookish Cs of fiction, with their pale skin and pale blue eyes and pale pedantic monologues. C was robust, with muscles and a suntan, a closely clipped black beard and thick black hair and eyebrows. He was an ex-New Scotland Yard superintendent, an ex-R.N. intelligence chief and a former amateur light-heavy-weight boxing champion of England. Perhaps he was more a fictional character than any of them.

Evans spent his time pottering about the flat, getting himself simple meals, drinking a little more than usual and reading. Two or three afternoons during the week he strolled round to the library and changed his books. He was now well on the mend and able to walk upright, enjoying the warm sunshine and the cold bracing air, and the fact that the BBC was continually mentioning that it was raining in Spain. Sara was wrong. London was better than Spain.

He thought it strange that there had been nothing in the papers about Hannifin's defection. But then it came in the morning press in a story date-lined *Moscow, Tuesday*, and put out by Tass News Agency. Tim's picture was on the front page.

Evans read one report completely and threw the others aside. It all seemed remote now, and far away. He bought the afternoon papers but Sara's article wasn't in. There was scathing comment about the British Secret Service from the feature and leader writers. He put the papers out of sight and left the radio and TV switched off. He was not that interested.

Evans said: 'I saw the article. I didn't read it.'

'He forgets we're well ahead on defections. We've five Russians to this one unfortunate mistake in over four years!' Control slapped the folded newspaper with the back of his hand.

Evans nodded. He poured water into C's whisky, then into his own. He was in pyjamas, dressing-gown and slippers. It was after ten o'clock and C had just arrived on his doorstep. His black Daimler stood down in the dark mews in a sudden downpour.

'This man Bennett uses this Hannifin thing as an excuse to rake over all the muck of the past!'

'I didn't read it.' Evans handed him a drink.

'Thanks. Here's luck, Mike.' In the office, C would have said 'Evans'.

Mike drank with him. They were both standing by the fireplace. C wore a healthy suntan and his beard was freshly trimmed. Beside him Evans looked small and pale.

'Listen to this about Fuchs and Nunn May!' C went on. He read: '"The real value to the Soviet Union was not the benefit Russia received from their scientific information but the psychological and propaganda value of their apprehension and capture by ourselves!" Well, any fool knows that! But what are we supposed to do if we find an enemy spy in our camp? Let him continue to feed our vital secrets to the enemy? Apparently, according to Bennett! Anyway, Mike, how *are* you?'

C was looking hard at him—hard into his face. And Evans met his eyes frankly. C liked Evans. He had a fighter's face that had taken blows, and a steady look in his eyes. He held his shoulders slightly forward like many class middle-weights he'd known.

C said softly: 'Tell me about it.'

Evans told him. He offered no excuses. He made no disparaging comment about Hannifin. What he said matched Towery's report and damned him as completely. C listened without interrupting. Evans was a field man, and field men didn't live lives that other people could understand. They often had to live in seedy surroundings. They had to win confidences and dishonour them. They had to lie and cheat, and often live double, even treble, lives. And occasionally they were faced with the necessity of having to kill someone in order to stay alive. The life they led took its toll. They didn't remain the same people. Sometimes melancholy and drink took them. Or a dreadful lassitude brought a glaze to their eyes. Whenever C saw this in a man he took him off the job at once, for it was the danger sign. It meant that drink or conscience or tension had slowed up his thinking and made him vulnerable. It was C's job to recognize the sickened soul, the crippled brain, to anticipate and head-off the crack-up before it happened. Sometimes, after a good rest and a change of surroundings, they came all the way back and became good spies again. If they didn't, you put them into a safe dead-end job in the Department, or else you gave them a pension and sent them out to grass to live with their memories until they died.

As Evans talked, C felt relieved. There was no dissipation beyond the normal, no glazed look. His speech was calm and straight-forward, logical and unconfused. No hang-up. There was no self-hatred or self-justification. He had come through his failure well. The only thing missing now was motivation.

To keep him talking C asked several questions.

'Why didn't you handle Eisendrath yourself?'

'It would have meant a different plan. More direct. I'd never have got close enough to him, let alone be invited to his home. Hannifin was a teacher. It was logical to set him up with the proper identity and let him attend the university.'

'Why was it necessary for you to go to Germany at such a vital time?'

Evans told him about his drive to Deggendorf, the two days of subterfuge, his cutting out by train. C nodded. He could see no flaw in the plan. It should have worked. The mistake had been made much earlier, with the choice of Hannifin. That was Evans's first and only mistake. He said so.

'But Hannifin *was* the plan!' Evans said. 'Without Hannifin or somebody like him it would have been a break-and-entry job, which could have had disastrous consequences. There was more in this operation than meets the eye!'

C looked at him curiously. 'What makes you say that?'

'Eisendrath is not the KGB. He is not Smersh. He's in a different league. Hannifin was a pawn in the game—or a casualty.'

'In what kind of game?'

'On another level.' Evans pointed to his head. 'Up here.'

C finished his drink and set his glass down firmly. 'Well, I just wanted to come and get a good look at you. I think you'll be all right.'

The two men looked squarely at each other.

C said: 'Yes. I *think* you'll be all right.'

Sara Collins's story hit the front page of the *Daily Mentor* the following morning. The headline read: SOVIET METHODS EXPOSED. It was sub-titled: HANNIFIN'S DEADLY GAME.

Evans smiled. He thought of the funny little girl with the freckles on her nose. BY SARA COLLINS. He thought of her leaving the hospital that night after their chat and going back to her room at the Kaiserhof and sitting down hunched over her portable typewriter and smoking cigarettes. He read what she had written.

While a tense and anxious world awaited the coming of daylight when its leaders would awaken in Vienna to work together for the peace of Europe, a man with a stocking stretched over his face skulked in the shadows of a basement stairway less than three hundred yards from the conference venue.

He was a paid servant of the Kremlin, and, stiletto in hand, he was carrying out his orders under the rules of the game that Russia has chosen to play in world affairs.

Three hours before, as the price which would ensure his future in the Soviet Union, Timothy Hannifin had told the KGB where they would find his former colleague, the British agent who had befriended him and inducted him into the Secret Service.

Shortly after midnight this agent, worried for Hannifin's safety, hurried out of the building into the dark street. The Soviet spy stealthily crept from his hiding place and plunged the stiletto into the agent's side and left him bleeding to death on the pavement.

By this time, Timothy Hannifin was safely aboard a plane bound for Warsaw on the first leg of his flight to Moscow.

This is how Hannifin defected.

The story went on to indict the British defector as a self-seeking opportunist and cold-blooded murderer. It insisted that Hannifin's statement in Moscow of his lofty ideals and his reasons for defecting were a hollow mockery. But, the story read, the individual was not to blame. The nations who employed such people and such methods were responsible. The world seemed to have gone back to the Europe of the Dark Ages.

As soon as Evans had read the story he expected the phone to ring, and it did. It was Cookie, C's diminutive secretary.

'Control would like to see you as soon as possible. Can you come in by taxi right away?'

Evans said he could.

When he was shown into the large green-and-white room overlooking St James's Place, C and Chauncey Bowes were there. Chauncey was tall, bald-headed, angular and pink-cheeked. He'd come into MI5 from psychological warfare late in the war. Both men were standing. The newspaper was spread out on the desk.

C tapped the article. 'Are you responsible for this?' he demanded.

Mike said: 'Partly.' He told them about Hannifin's letter to Sara Collins. 'But she wasn't buying. She saw through him. She guessed that he'd relied on her being a newspaper woman and that she wouldn't be able to resist publishing his letter. It was a sop to all the fellow travellers in the world. She wouldn't have it. But she wanted to write the story and asked me for some facts.'

'And you gave them to her?'

'She knew most of it already—from Hannifin. I told her the details of the attack on me.'

There was a pause. Evans was mystified at their reaction. It wasn't at all hostile, as he'd expected. Giving facts to a newspaper reporter was the blackest deed an agent could commit. Chauncey Bowes was looking at C like a red setter waiting for its master to throw him a stick. C looked at Evans with hard boring eyes. Then he turned to Bowes.

'All right. He's yours.'

4

On the following Monday morning Mike Evans put in an appearance at the Department, long enough to give a month's notice, in writing. Then he sullenly cleaned out his office and left. Next morning he showed up in a tiny brown office on the second floor adjacent to Central Registry. He'd already been removed from the books of the field department and did not encourage the *camaraderie* of the other field men who dropped into London. Those who tried shrugged and left him well alone. Bad luck. They felt sorry for him. It could happen to anyone. And he'd been given a raw deal over Hannifin's defection. But if he chose to sit in his office all day and lick his wounds there was nothing they could do about it.

Actually, Evans was not licking his wounds. He was secretly writing a book.

He'd planned it as a documentary account, written from inside the SIS, of Kim Philby's double game between MI5 and the MVD. And his plan was to sell it to the highest bidder.

In order not to arouse suspicion within the sub-section, he called for many other files on other topics. Whenever he wanted items photo-copied he'd put them in the open bottom drawer of his desk, shine a reading lamp onto them and photograph them with a miniature camera designed exactly for this purpose.

After the first week he began to steal three afternoons a week, leaving the office at a quarter to one and not coming back. Fanning, the head of the sub-section, noted this, and so did some of the clerks. A few of them had seen him, a solitary drinker, standing at the end of the bar in a nearby pub. But he was able to get home by three and work through until the early hours. And in the morning he would arrive late at the office, his eyes red-rimmed with tiredness.

On Tuesday of the third week, Fanning sent a message asking him to go and see him. Evans went into Fanning's office.

The sub-section head, a small wiry man with a scrawny neck popping out of a high stiff collar, closed the door carefully behind him and invited him to sit down. As soon as he was sitting opposite he looked at Evans with cold hard eyes.

'Just what are you up to, Mr Evans?'

'What are you talking about?'

'Why are you so interested in Philby?'

'What are you talking about?'

Fanning had a list before him showing file numbers and dates. 'I've a list of files you've been calling for.'

'What about them?'

The two men stared at each other for several seconds.

Fanning said: 'I've taken the trouble to check the amount of work you've done on the record sheets. You've scarcely touched them. You've been doing something else. Something connected with Philby.'

'Don't be ridiculous!'

'Well, I've sent a copy of this list upstairs. I thought they'd better see it.'

Evans stood up.

Fanning said: 'And, Mr Evans, for the rest of your time in my section would you mind not going out for hours at a time? It's very bad for the discipline of the rest of my staff. Just because you've had a so-called glamour job for some years——'

'Go to hell!' Evans said quietly and walked out.

He went to his office, folded up some sheets of writing and put them in his pocket, put on his coat, took his hat from the peg and walked out.

He didn't go to the office after that. His final cheque was paid into his bank. He was now an ex-member of SIS, and one not held in very high odour.

But he was happy. His book made good progress. He had the great advantage of having worked with Philby for three years, first when he was in charge of the Iberian section of Department V and later when he was organizing a new section to counter Russian espionage. Evans was honest and dispassionate and gave Philby credit for his motives. But Philby was a spy. Philby was the enemy. He worked inside the SIS as a trusted operative. The documents he used to support the chilling story of how Philby eliminated Thornhill in a bitter internal power struggle made the blood run cold. Shortly after two o'clock one morning Evans typed:

One afternoon I drove to the ugly sprawling Edwardian house on the borders of Ashdown forest. I wanted to see Philby and ask him the nagging questions that were in my mind. I rang the bell and heard it ring hollowly. I looked through the side panels that framed the door and could see that the floor was littered with mail and advertising brochures. I closed the gate and went back to my car and drove back to Crowborough, mystified. I didn't know it then, but Kim Philby had already left for Beirut. He was on his way to Moscow.

Evans tore the sheet from the typewriter and added it to the pile of four hundred pages. Then he typed the title-page:

THE PHILBY STORY
BY MICHAEL EVANS

One evening Evans had a ring from a man who introduced himself as Bentleigh Stringer, a brother-in-law of Chris West whom Evans knew from Naval Intelligence. Stringer invited him to have lunch with him the following day. Evans was mystified but he agreed.

They met in the foyer of the Dorchester at twelve-thirty. Stringer turned out to be an imposing pear shape in a tailored grey flannel suit and a Homburg. He strode in out of the sunshine five minutes late, looked around majestically and spotted Evans. He came across to meet him.

'You're Michael Evans.' He said it as a fact.

Evans said: 'You must be Chris West's brother-in-law.'

'That's right.' They shook hands. 'A little something before we eat, shall we?' Stringer ushered him into the cocktail bar. 'What will you have? I'm a champers man myself. I find it suits every occasion. Don't you?' He gave the impression of being immensely pleased with himself and of wanting to share his happiness with others.

'Scotch for me, thanks. With water.'

Evans hadn't taken to Stringer at first sight. He found it hard to tolerate youngish men with soft faces and flabby figures. He sized the big man up and knew that one quick short-arm jab into that capacious gut would have him writhing on the floor in two seconds. It was automatic for Evans to measure every man he met and to look for his weakest point. Things like this were second nature to an agent. And the survival habit went further. It even drew his eyes to the long mirror across the bar to run along the faces of the other customers. He always looked for the loner, the man who stood alone, unnoticed among the knots of drinkers. He saw one now. About five places along the bar. A clean-cut compact man with a nondescript face. He was fortyish, dressed expensively in navy blue, with a pale blue shirt and a maroon tie. He appeared to be absorbed in the contents of a tall glass. Now and then he would look at his wrist-watch and turn towards the entrance.

'Just to be businesslike,' Stringer was saying, having paid for the drinks. He drew an embossed card from his lizardskin wallet and put it on the bar.

'Thanks.' Evans picked up the card and read: *Bentleigh Stringer and Sheila Swann. Authors' Agents.* It gave an address in Albemarle Street.

'Chris tells me you've just left the Service. Cheers, old man. Nice to meet you.'

'Cheers.' They drank.

'Well, maybe Chris is some kind of catalyst. Or maybe he's talking through his hat. I don't know. But something he said over the week-end prompted me to ring you.' Evans looked at him. 'I'm an authors' agent.'

Evans nodded. He wasn't making it very easy.

Stringer said: 'I believe I could sell your memoirs—should you decide to write them, that is.'

'That's interesting.'

'I believe I could get a top price for them.'

'What about syndication in the press?'

'That goes without saying.'

They went into lunch. As Stringer ushered him into the vast dining-hall he paused to whisper a little joke into the ear of the *maître d'hôtel*, then introduced Mr Evans. A spry grey-haired waiter glided ahead and escorted them to their table.

The ordering was a serious business and took time. Bentleigh made you feel it was worthy of a man's greatest concentration for the day. Evans chose oysters and a grilled steak, medium rare. The table wine was a still red. Sitting opposite his host, Evans saw that what had once been a pleasant boyish face was still handsome enough, feature by feature. But now it was pink and rounded by expense-account living. A once likably pugnacious dimpled chin was now heavy-jowled and merged with a thickening neck.

Over oysters, Stringer said with studied detachment: 'Does the idea make any sense to you?'

Evans nodded. 'Very much. As a matter of fact, I've been fiddling with a book.'

Stringer's eyes widened with anticipation. 'You have?'

'Yes.'

They ate in silence for a time.

Evans said casually: 'It brings to light certain new facts about Kim Philby.' He went on eating.

'I see. That's interesting.'

Evans wondered whether the name Philby meant anything

to an authors' agent. Apparently it did, for Stringer said presently: 'I'm more than interested. When may I see it?'

'I'll let you know.'

They were well into the second course, with the glasses refilled, when Stringer said: 'Come to think of it, this is quite a coincidence, particularly with Philby on the other side of the Iron Curtain.'

'How do you mean?'

'My brother-in-law has a greater insight into these things than I ever gave him credit for!'

'In what way?'

'The most successful titles I've handled this year and last year have come from the Soviet Union.'

Evans looked at him, astounded. 'You mean—from the underground writers?'

'That's exactly what I mean.' He threw out two titles airily. '*When Tyrants Seem To Kiss*, by Godlovsky. Fotoyev's *The Pelican*.' He shrugged to infer he could have gone on for hours.

Evans nodded. 'I've read them. But how on earth do *you* contact the underground? How do you receive their manuscripts?'

Stringer looked round the dining-room and leaned toward his guest. 'I shouldn't tell you this, but you've been in the Service all this time. I go to West Berlin every month and meet the underground's representative. He passes the manuscripts to me.'

'So in a way, you're a sort of Scarlet Pimpernel of literature?'

Stringer flushed with pleasure, delighted at the association. 'Well, I suppose I am, if it comes to that!' He raised his glass and drank appreciatively. 'This is a surprisingly good red!'

Evans asked: 'But how do you know which day of the month to meet him?'

'Oh, that's pre-arranged. It's the tenth of each month.'

'Then you were in West Berlin last week?'

'Of course.'

'But where do you meet?'

'Oh, we have a *pension* we rent only for the purpose of the meeting.'

'Always the same rendezvous?'

'Yes. Modest little place. Very respectable. No one would suspect what goes on there.'

'And your contact? What is he? A Russian?'

'Yes.'

'But you don't *stay* at the *pension*?'

'Oh, good Lord, no! I stay at the Hilton. I'm quite a regular there. They even make sure I get the particular suite I like on the fifth floor!' He leaned across the table and said in a low voice: 'He rings me on the tenth of each month—after midday —and tells me that my laundry is ready. As soon as I receive his call I go round to the *pension* and wait for him.'

'How do you go?'

'By taxi. How else?'

'And how long has this been going on?'

'Seven months.'

'Interesting. You should have been in the Secret Service, Bentleigh.'

'That's what Chris says!'

Stringer restrained himself and refused the banana flambé. They had cheese and biscuits, then coffee, liqueurs and cigars. Then they went back to the cocktail bar for a final drink. Stringer was now flushed with food, alcohol and success. The bar was almost deserted and Evans noted that the solitary drinker was still there.

After the drink, Stringer and Evans stepped out into the foyer and strolled toward the glass doors.

Stringer said: 'When shall I see the manuscript?'

'I'll let you know.'

At the entrance, Evans hesitated. 'Thanks for the lunch. I have one or two phone calls to make.'

They shook hands. Stringer went out onto the pavement and turned left to the cab rank.

As Evans turned toward the telephones he noticed the lone drinker walking purposefully out of the hotel.

5

Evans was amazed at the speed with which things happened after that. Within three days of the manuscript being placed in Bentleigh Stringer's hands, the rights had been bought by Brayne-Watts, the trans-Atlantic publishing combine, and they sold the serial rights immediately to newspapers throughout the world. A Sunday paper bought them for Great Britain and set in motion a massive publicity campaign to launch the opening instalment. Evans had signed a contract accepting an initial figure equal to ten years' salary and had been paid by cheque. Bentleigh Stringer had made himself a sizable commission.

Michael Evans's name was featured in the press and on television, and overnight he had become one of the most controversial and vilified people in England. Members of the public wrote to the editors of the London dailies expressing their disgust at Evans's opportunism and downright disloyalty, and he was castigated on the leader pages of rival newspapers. One of them offered him a job as a foreign correspondent, and when he turned it down the same paper attacked him, labelling him 'The Man Who Sold Out The Secret Service'. And this phrase stuck. But it didn't affect his earning power. One national daily offered him a job to write for them as 'Our Man On The Spot'. Because of the increasing tension between East and West Germany his first assignment was West Berlin.

He reported all this to Chauncey Bowes, who told him:

'That's right. C arranged all this at the top. Things don't usually happen this fast. But we want you in Berlin as soon as possible—certainly before Stringer gets there on the tenth.'

On Wednesday, Chauncey rang him. 'We've got to have a talk.'

'Department S? What does it stand for?'

'That we don't know,' Chauncey said. 'Maybe "soul", but the Marxists don't believe in the soul, do they?'

'What is it? How does it operate?'

'Department S began as an internal instrument which used the Soviet Writers' Union to pressure its members into spying on other members and reporting anyone who was writing underground literature. But then the underground got better organized and established their own secret publications that circulated inside Russia, and their own pipeline to Western publishers.'

Evans nodded.

'But Department S is now operating on a world-wide basis in an effort to combat the psychological and propaganda effects of the underground writers.'

'A Soviet version of the USIA?'

'No. They already have Tass and other services. Department S starts where they finish.' He drew a sheet of paper from his pocket, unfolded it and read: '"I was taken by night to the Lubyanka prison and ordered to write a report against an American diplomat to the effect that he subjected me and other Soviet citizens to malicious brain-washing."' He refolded the paper. 'There are more than thirty of these examples in Vishniak's report on Department S.'

'Who is Vishniak?'

'Rodya Vishniak. A former writer attached to Department S. He defected to us a week ago. We have him under wraps.'

'How much could he tell you about S?'

'Not very much. It is run by General Mikhail Zadikov, a former head of armed services information. His chief-of-operations is Alex Kovarsky, a former secretary of the Russian Writers' Union, and later on the staff of Smersh specifically to work against the underground writers. Kovarsky is the most dangerous man in Department S. He's the man you'll have to watch out for.'

'Alex Kovarsky.'

'Yes. We also have the names of several of their writers and operators—including Tim Hannifin.' He dropped the name like a stone in a fish-pond.

Evans looked at him steadily. 'Hannifin's with S?'

'Yes. Vishniak says he's very close to Kovarsky.'

After a pause, Evans said: 'Stringer is being followed. Did you know that?'

Bowes nodded. 'Tyagen. He's a cipher clerk at the Russian Embassy. He's been following Stringer since his last visit to West Berlin.'

'So Kovarsky knows Stringer's been in touch with me?'

'Naturally. And no doubt he's waiting avidly for your Philby story.'

'What about Stringer's contact in West Berlin?'

'His name is Danilov. He works for a printer.'

'How does the pipeline operate?'

'They smuggle the manuscripts to Danilov as and when they can. On the tenth of each month Danilov brings them to Stringer at the *pension* in Schaperstrasse.'

'Has the underground been contacted?'

'Not yet. But Walkley's made contact with Danilov.'

'Walkley?'

'Our man in West Berlin. You'll be working with him.'

'Tell me about him.'

'Derek Walkley. He's twenty-eight. Oxford. A bit of a long-hair. A poet. Seems to be just the man to gain the confidence of the underground writers.'

'Where'd you find him?'

'Working for Amnesty. He is dedicated to helping the oppressed writers behind the Iron Curtain. He speaks Russian and German. And he's good with a pistol and at unarmed combat.'

'Sounds all right.' Evans knocked his pipe out on the grate. 'What does he know about *me*?'

'Everything. He knows the plot. It couldn't be otherwise.'

'How will I contact him?'

'He'll contact *you*.'

Evans nodded. After a pause he said: 'How did Vishniak defect?'

'He was sent to Prague to work against the underground journalists and writers. We spotted him for a mixed-up liberal and put Pravja onto him. One night he told Pravja he wanted to defect and Pravja brought him across the border at Liberec and got him through to East Berlin and handed him over to Karl. Karl got him across the Wall.'

'Karl still effective? That's worth knowing.'

Bowes nodded with a smirk. 'He's a thorn in Arkov's side.'

Evans considered this information. 'There's a very real angle. Any other Department S defector could be a trap set by Arkov.'

'Yes. You'll have to keep that in mind.'

'And S's Chief of Operations? Kovarsky? What do you want done with him?'

'Disgraced or exterminated. He deserves no one's mercy. It will be your decision.'

'And Hannifin?'

'Leave him alone. Killing Hannifin won't achieve anything.'

The Viscount touched down gently on the runway of Tempelhof Airport. Two seconds later a burst of reverse power checked its rush. Then it was turning and the plane's four propellers wheeled to a stop as it reached the busy terminal buildings.

Evans nodded pleasantly to the stewardess and carried his typewriter through the passport check into Customs. He waited for his suitcase and overnight bag to come off the plane.

As he was standing there, a hand took his elbow gently and turned him round.

'Hallo, Evans.'

He was looking into a small smiling face with enormous blue-tinted spectacles.

'Hallo, Collins,' he said.

And the next moment Sara Collins was standing on tip-toe hugging and kissing him like a long-lost sweetheart.

He put down his typewriter, held her away from him so that he could see the freckles on her nose. Then he kissed her lightly on the lips.

'That's for your article,' he told her with a smile.

She said: 'That's the first time I've ever seen you smile, Evans.' The 'Evans' sounded like a term of endearment.

As soon as he was through Customs and Currency and had located his luggage, she steered him to a waiting taxi.

When the car was gliding out of the airport, the driver turned and asked politely in guttural English: 'Where to, sir?'

Before Evans could reply, Sara said: 'The Europa, please.'

Evans looked at her questioningly.

She told him: 'We newspaper people have our own underground.'

After a time she put her arm through his and looked earnestly into his face.

'Did you live?'

He nodded. 'Did you?'

She smiled and said: 'You should see me now!'

Evans vaguely noticed a brown Renault 16 in the rear-vision mirror. It was too far back for him to see that the driver was a young man with longish dark brown hair, and that his face wore a look of sullen contempt.

They dined at the Schischko, a tiny Balkan restaurant on Wilmersdorferstrasse. Balkan rugs and trinkets adorned the walls, and waiters decked out in colourful Yugoslavian sashes served *schaschlik* with rice, Balkan salad and garnishes which were heavy with raw onion. They were drinking Ouzo, chased by mouthfuls of ice-water. There was a strong bite under the sickly anisette taste and Evans felt the drink light a small fire down his throat and in his stomach.

After the frustrating stretch of hospitalization and convalescence, followed by the weeks of writing and concentrating on the details of a manuscript, and of surreptitious file-hunting in Fanning's hole-in-the-wall office, Evans felt a relief at being his own master. He was here in West Berlin, and only a few hundred yards away was the Wall and the Russian-controlled sector of the city, and all around the tiny enclave was a hostile East Germany, and all the way east and north were the Warsaw Pact countries and the Soviet Union, 'where the guard dogs howl all night', as a spy author had once written. And for some reason the realization gave him a pang of pleasure and excitement.

She told him about journalists; the routine of press conferences, getting news hand-outs, arranging exclusive interviews, looking for news angles, how they worked together but scooped each other, how they spent their spare time in foreign cities.

'You'll have to meet some of them,' she said. 'Come over to Bill Herrara's tomorrow evening. It's our Saturday chinwag.'

'Who's Bill Herrara?'

'My chief.'

'Count me in. Where and when?'

'I'll pick you up at eight and take you along.'

'Thanks. Now I'm going to take you home.'

As they stepped out into Wilmersdorferstrasse he said: 'How will your journalists regard my book? Will they think I'm the man who sold out the Secret Service?'

'Probably. But they won't hold it against you. To a newspaperman no fact is sacrosanct. If it's true it should be published. They'll judge you on your professionalism, and whether or not you've split an infinitive. Have you?'

'I wouldn't know one if I fell over it.'

He hailed a passing cab. He gave instructions to the driver. The car took off down the street. Somewhere behind them, he vaguely heard the sound of a car starting up.

As they neared her hotel she asked: 'Would you like to come up for a drink?'

Evans had Walkley on his mind. 'No, thanks, Collins. Unpacking, you know,' he said lamely. 'Must get settled in.'

She sighed. 'I'm going to grow on you like a wart. It's my only chance.'

The cab pulled up for her to get out. She turned to look at him. 'You've got such a tough knocked-about face, Evans. Whoever pushed that nose on one side like that?'

'Sugar Ray.'

She kissed him on the cheek and got out and he watched her run up the steps to the hotel lobby, turn and wave, then disappear. He told the driver to take him to the Hotel Europa.

As he was paying the driver he noticed a black DKW pull into the kerb about a hundred yards behind. He went into the hotel and inquired for his key. There were no messages and he took the elevator to the sixth floor.

He stepped out onto the thickly carpeted corridor, turned right and found his room—number 612. He inserted the key, clicked back the bolt and eased the door inwards.

A reading lamp was on and a man sat relaxed in the upholstered chair by the window, smoking a cigarette.

'Hallo, cock.' He took the cigarette from his mouth and sent out a stream of smoke. His face was wreathed in a twisted grin.

6

As Evans closed the door and stepped into the room the man said:

'I'm Walkley.'

Evans turned on the main lights and looked at him, hard.

'I'm glad you are. How did you get in?'

The young man patted his pocket. 'My Pringle special.' This referred to Horace Pringle, the SIS equipment specialist responsible for kitting the field men. Walkley was just under six feet, with too much hair for Evans's liking, and he had a lean sensitive face with pallid, rather pimply, skin that spoke of coffee lounges and long-playing records.

Evans stood a yard away from him and said quietly: 'Don't ever enter my room like that again.'

'I wanted to catch up with you.' Walkley spoke insolently, regarding Evans with heavy-lidded eyes. There was no mistaking the drawling inflexion he put on the words 'catch up'.

Evans said: 'Spies should never act like spies.'

'What *should* they act like?'

They outstared each other for a few seconds. Evans stroked his chin and turned away. He went to the luggage rack and opened his case. Silently, methodically, he began to unpack his things and place them in the drawers of the dressing-table and in the wardrobe. Having finished the case he unzipped his overnight bag and unpacked it, laying out his pyjamas and dressing-gown on the bedspread.

Walkley sat regarding him with eyes that gradually showed

annoyance. He stubbed out his cigarette then lit another.

Evans undressed, hung his suit on a hanger and put it in the wardrobe, put his underclothes on a chair and went into the bathroom. After a lengthy shower he came out drying himself, then put on his pyjamas, dressing-gown and slippers. Then he sat on the bed and began to fill his pipe.

Walkley said: 'I went out to the airport to meet you six hours ago!'

Evans nodded, poking down the tobacco with his thumb. 'You were in a brown Renault.'

Walkley looked slightly jolted. 'Yes.'

'That was a mistake.' Evans lit a match, put it to the bowl and drew in the flame several times. He shook out the match. 'If *I* noticed you trailing me, someone else could have.' He looked steadily at Walkley. 'And coming here tonight and breaking into my room was just plain bloody stupid!'

'I don't think so.'

'You've seen too many spy films. The procedure was for you to ring me, using the name "Redrop". We would take it from there.'

Walkley shrugged. He looked round the room intensely. He said presently: 'I wanted to see you urgently!'

'All right.' Evans stood up. He said quietly: 'Look, Walkley. I have a job to do. So have you. It's essential that we trust each other, understand each other and depend on each other. It would also be an advantage if we liked each other.'

Walkley stood up, his mouth working with annoyance. 'Look. I went out to the airport because I wanted to see you urgently. Then I rang as arranged, but you were still out! You'd gone to dinner with the girl who'd met you at the airport!'

'So?'

'Well, look. Things are happening! I've got to go to East Berlin tomorrow and I wanted to talk to you and——' He broke off, looking sullenly at the floor.

'Well, go on with it. What's troubling you?'

'Nothing.'

There was a pause. Evans took his pipe from his mouth and held it in his left hand. He said quietly: 'I think you'd better tell me.'

Walkley made no sign that he had heard. His jaws were clamped shut. Evans turned and switched off the main lights, then the reading lamp. He went to the window in the darkness and pulled aside the curtains slightly.

'You see that black DKW? That belongs to one of the men who's following me. Maybe there's someone following *you*. If there isn't now, there will be.'

Walkley edged to the window and looked down. He said nothing. Evans closed the curtains then switched on the light.

He pulled back the bed-clothes ready for bed.

'Now either tell me what you came here for or get the hell out of my room!'

After a few seconds, Walkley said: 'I'm sorry.'

'Well, that's a start.'

'I've been waiting three days to see you. And when I went out to the airport and found I couldn't——'

Evans held up a bottle of Scotch from the dressing-table. 'Drink?'

'Thanks.'

'You know about Danilov?'

'Yes. You've made contact with him?'

'That's right. I've alerted him that he may be in danger.'

'Is he being followed?'

'He's quite certain he's not. He thinks he's quite safe, in fact.'

'Tell me about your meeting with him,' Evans said.

'Oh, I've met him more than once.'

'How many times?'

'Three. The first time I rang the printery and asked for Herr Danilov. I gave the name "Heiskell". When he came to the phone I said in Russian: "Mr Danilov. My name means nothing to you. But I know why you are in West Berlin." There was a pause on the line. He must have been pretty shocked. He said: "I do not know what you are talking about. You must have the wrong party."' Walkley put down his glass while he lit a cigarette. 'I said: "You meet a man named Stringer once a month." He said at once: "You want to tell me something? Where can I see you?" I told him to go to a coffee shop near the Eduscho and carry something. He agreed and said he had to deliver a parcel of printing to a shop in the Ku-Damm. It would be quarto-size and wrapped in green paper with a white label and the word "Wienerwald", the name of the printery, on it.'

Evans listened, watching Walkley carefully. Despite their bad beginning the younger man had thawed out a little, though there was still a reserve between them.

Walkley went on: 'Well, he showed up and we met briefly. I gave him the address of my *pension* and a spare key. He called on me about ten that evening. We had a chat and I convinced him that I was his friend and the friend of the Soviet underground. I showed him my Amnesty reference, which is a very good one. That did it, I think. He even read some of my poetry. Anyway, I asked him a lot of questions and he answered them. I think he was relieved at meeting someone else this side of the Wall besides Stringer.'

'How does he feel about Stringer?'

'He's not happy. In fact none of them are.'

'None of them?'

'The underground. But Stringer gets results for them. He advises on the manuscripts, arranges the translations, has them published, and gets the money paid into an account in Zurich. They have nearly half a million pounds sterling in it so far.'

'Well, why don't they trust him?'

'They think he may be a bad security risk. Anyway, they prefer his partner, Sheila Swann. It was she who opened up the first contact with them—in Helsinki.'

Evans said drily: 'Stringer omitted to tell me. Well, how far have you got? As you know, Stringer is due in West Berlin again on Sunday for the next rendezvous with Danilov.'

'Yes. And Danilov wants me to meet the underground before then. He's passed a message to his contact across the Wall and it's all set for me to go. I'm going tomorrow.'

'Who are you meeting?'

'A man named Jonas. Danilov thinks they want to meet me and discuss the whole thing before Stringer arrives.'

'What time are you going?'

'About nine. I'll spend the whole day sight-seeing and getting the lie of the land.'

Evans nodded. 'What's the set-up for the meeting?'

'Danilov has given me a ticket to the opera. It's a reserved seat, of course. I have to wear a red tie.'

'A red tie? At the opera?'

Walkley nodded, grinning. 'Nothing like Vienna or London apparently. The Socialist paradise makes no impositions like black ties and white shirts. I'm to wear a red tie and have a book on my lap.'

'What book?'

'*And Quiet Flows the Don.*'

'The underground has a sense of humour.' Evans was remembering that its author, Mikhail Sholokov, had damned all Soviet writers who ate Soviet bread but served Western bourgeois masters by sending their works to them through secret channels. He asked: 'What precautions have you taken? Or will you take?'

Walkley produced a card from his wallet. 'I'm a paid-up member of the World Writers' Union and the British Writers for Peace.'

'Why are you living in West Berlin?'

'Writing a prose-poem on the life and times of Adolf Hitler, condemning his nationalism, of course.' He added: 'I really *am* doing this.'

'Good. What else?'

'Well, what do *you* suggest?'

46

'You can register your name with the American M.P.'s at Checkpoint Charlie and tell them the approximate time you expect to return. If you don't show up they'll take action to find you.'

Walkley looked doubtful. 'That could be difficult. I assume the underground will want to see me after the show. And maybe we'll have supper and talk for an hour or two. Anyway, I'll leave my name at the checkpoint.'

'And get them to ring *me* if you're not through by, say, four a.m.'

'Right.'

'Whatever you do, don't stay overnight. That could be dangerous. Even if it's four before you're through, come back to the checkpoint and tell the Vopos you were backstage with some of the cast of the opera.'

Walkley nodded. Evans poured another drink.

Before he left, Walkley said: 'The girl who met you at the airport.'

Evans grinned. 'She's still on your mind, isn't she?'

'Who is she?'

'Sara Collins, an American newspaper woman. She works for a syndicate. She's not Mata Hari.'

Walkley nodded. 'She wrote that article about Hannifin.'

'Right.'

'Well, unless you hear to the contrary, I'll cross tomorrow morning and return Sunday in the early hours.'

'You'd better give me your West Berlin address in case anything goes wrong. We'd hate for posterity to lose that prose-poem.'

Walkley gave him an address in Wilmersdorf and Evans wrote it down in a small notebook. Evans asked for the registration number of Walkley's Renault. Walkley told him and Evans wrote it down.

Evans said: 'Well, good luck, Derek.'

They shook hands and Walkley left.

Watching from the window of the darkened room, Evans saw the Renault drive off. The DKW remained where it was.

47

7

Bill Herrara turned out to be a handsome pale-faced roly-poly American with tremendous energy and an enormous appetite. His guests were Jay Burchard of the *Washington Mail* and Scott Cory, the West German head of the United States Information Agency. When Evans arrived with Sara on his arm he was given a warm welcome by the U.P. chief, who called him 'Mike' right off.

It was a pleasant evening of the special barbed conversation of international journalists and Bourbon on the rocks. Evans did not object to it. He enjoyed the ribbing the USIA man came in for. Burchard brought up the subject of a recent questionnaire sent to all United States diplomats in Eastern Europe asking what sort of government they thought the people of the Warsaw Pact countries would choose if they had a free choice.

'And the answer was Dubček-type socialism!' Burchard said, and the others laughed.

Cory nodded, showing his chagrin. 'And my chief, Frank Shakespeare, was hopping mad!'

They laughed again.

The USIA man said seriously: 'Well, let's face it. We've got a problem. The majority of books written today tend to be written by people on the liberal side because they're more articulate. We just can't find writers on the other side, apart from Rayner Nash.'

Herrara was serving the drinks. 'Scott thinks the best way

to fight for the American cause would be to put gung-ho Kiwanis boosters into all the Communist countries!'

'Well, I want to beat the bastards down, no kidding!' Cory said. 'And I don't care whether it takes the liberal or conservative viewpoint to do it! I'm a pragmatist!'

The ribbing went on until it became half serious. Everybody had his say.

When Burchard said something that got under his skin, Cory said pugnaciously: 'Look! There are people in the USIA who are soft on Communism, and I regard that as bad!'

Evans said: 'Yes. But there are writers in the Soviet who are soft on Freedom.'

Sara said: 'And they're liberals too!'

Herrara laughed and everyone talked at once.

Sara made the supper, and it was easy to see that her boss thought she was the greatest thing since the automat. The party broke up about one o'clock and Burchard dropped Sara and Evans at their hotels in his 'Thunderbird'.

Evans awoke abruptly as the telephone gave one sharp ring. He switched on the light and lifted the receiver.

The night clerk said: 'Herr Evans?'

'Yes.'

'A call for you, sir.'

'Thanks.'

An American voice came in the line. 'Mister Evans. This is Checkpoint Charlie. A Mister Walkley left a message with us yesterday morning that if he hadn't come through by four o'clock this morning we were to ring you, sir.'

'That's right.'

'Well, sir. It's half past four, and I'm just ringing to say there's been no sign of Mister Walkley so far.'

'Well, thank you.'

'You're welcome.'

The line went dead.

For several minutes Evans lay thinking. Perhaps he shouldn't be unduly worried. Walkley might have been delayed. But the thought didn't sit very well. He got out of bed and rang the night clerk and asked him to order a cab. When he left the hotel and entered the cab he noticed that the DKW was nowhere to be seen. Even spies had to sleep sometime. He asked the driver to take him to Checkpoint Charlie.

Bentleigh Stringer stared out of the window.

Danilov was late.

Stringer's gaze was riveted on the cold white street below the *pension*. Occasional vehicles hissed past on Schaperstrasse. The busy bustling Ku-Damm was only four blocks away, but in this street of ugly grey apartment buildings there was an aura of solitude. West Berlin lay beneath a film of powdered snow and the narrow lane that ran away from the *pension* was deserted.

Danilov would appear shortly at the mouth of the lane, a small rather forlorn figure in a rumpled grey-green duffel-coat, bespectacled, bearded, indecisive, looking rather like a Dostoyevski character.

As with his previous seven visits, their rendezvous was at the Pension Janssen in Schaperstrasse. Stringer always hired the same room for two days just for the meeting, which would take no more than an hour. The building had a deceptively ugly façade of greyish stucco, but inside it was a restored townhouse with rococo panelling, carved newel posts and large baroque doors. The *pension* was run by a friendly Danish woman, and her rooms were filled with old-fashioned family furniture. One of the reasons Bentleigh liked this room was the large Renoir nude over the bed. On raw days like today Frau Janssen lit the oil burner to warm the place before he arrived.

Bentleigh Stringer had to admit that these monthly jaunts were the high peak of his life. He liked the aura of intrepid 'cloak and dagger' activity that was now synonymous with his name in literary circles. He smiled smugly when he thought of his wife's parting 'Take care, darling,' as he'd said goodbye that morning before entering the waiting cab that would take him to Heathrow Airport. There'd been no mistaking the hero-worship in her glowing eyes.

There was no doubt, he thought warmly, that this new and immensely lucrative activity had paid off in tremendous dividends. More important, it had added a new dimension to his personality. He had become, as his new client Michael Evans had so aptly remarked, a sort of Pimpernel of the literary world. Yes. It was nice to be Bentleigh Stringer. And here he was, in West Berlin once again, waiting for Danilov, his contact with the literary underground.

The only thing that galled Bentleigh Stringer was that his partner, Sheila Swann, had been the one to get the firm onto this profitable 'underground literature' thing—just over two years ago in Helsinki. Sheila was an idealist and his mistress. She had gone to Helsinki that summer to collect names of world-famous writers and artists for a petition against the imprisonment and persecution of writers behind the Iron Curtain. Privately, Bentleigh had no doubts in his mind that Sheila had lived with the young Russian writer and translator, Yuri Nubrov, who had contacted her there. It was Nubrov who had secretively shown her the Godlovsky manuscript, *When Tyrants Seem To Kiss*. She'd brought it back to London in her vanity case. Brayne-Watts had snapped it up.

The first hard-cover edition of *Tyrants* became an immediate triumph which Bentleigh and Sheila toasted in champagne and celebrated with a week at the Don Pepe in Marbella. Overnight it became a bestseller on both sides of the Atlantic. A succession of reprints quickly followed, and it topped *Time*'s bestseller list five weeks running. Almost simultaneously there were the paperback editions, serializations, film rights, a Broadway play based on its characters. Bentleigh Stringer and Sheila Swann added an Inc. They had arrived—with Sheila, formerly his mistress-secretary, now indisputably and uncomfortably his aggressive and demanding equal partner. Fortunately, he'd been able to persuade her to leave London to open and manage the New York office.

Tyrants was followed by *The Pelican* by Sergei Fotoyev, which was also translated and brought to light by Yuri Nubrov, and smuggled back from Helsinki in the false bottom of Sheila's specially made 'cloak and dagger' vanity case. Then *The Newborn*, by Igor Ladikov. Bentleigh and Sheila now owned a Silver Cloud each. Bentleigh had moved with his wife, Dorothy, to a charming town-house in Knightsbridge. Their two children were now in exclusive boarding schools. And Sheila commuted regularly between London and New York.

Bentleigh thought of Sheila now, elegant even in nudity. Efficient, driving, dedicated, even ruthless, during office hours, but between sun-down and sun-up a little-girl-lost, insecure, hungry for his passion, for the feel of his arms around her naked back, for the touch of his hands. The image of her kindled a sudden spark that made him want to fly to New York that very afternoon and surprise her. But he knew he would never do that. He might catch her in bed with a brand new playwright. He preferred to leave things the way they were.

A shadow crossed his mind, as it had done several times this morning during the flight. He felt a fleeting premonition that his luck wouldn't hold, that something would go wrong this trip. And now he got a twinge of conscience as he saw himself on a plane between London and New York a fortnight before, talking himself silly to a girl called Ruth, telling her about his hotshot activities on behalf of the Soviet underground writers. Why didn't he learn to shut his mouth? Anyway, to hell with it.

He'd never forgotten the feeling of disaster that had swept him when Nubrov disappeared—when he vanished in Helsinki. He went out to buy some milk one morning and that was the last Sheila saw of him. He simply disappeared from the face of the earth. And suddenly, the source of a dozen gold-plated uranium eggs had gone.

He remembered the morning in March of this year when a 'Personal and Confidential' letter arrived on his desk. The post-mark showed that it had been posted in Paris the day before. It was addressed to Sheila Swann. He opened it and read:

Dear Miss Swann:

Your agency's specialized handling of the works of several of my friends has been mentioned to me many times.

I have in my possession a dynamic piece of writing by one of my closest friends, and I would like you to see it.

Would it be possible for you to come to Paris? You can contact me through Georges Daunou.

It was signed: Ivan Danilov

Daunou was a small-time *entrepreneur* with a tiny office in Avenue de Wagram. This was where Stringer had met Danilov nine months earlier. Bentleigh smiled at the memory of that first meeting with the Russian. Danilov had appeared plainly disappointed when he'd turned up in Paris in place of Sheila. Possibly he'd heard from Nubrov of Sheila's charms. He appeared suspicious and reluctant to deal with anyone but Sheila. However, Daunou, pre-oiled with the promise of future business, managed to save the day and sell Bentleigh's character and abilities to an only slightly mollified Danilov. Obviously, the Soviet literary underground had set great store by Sheila.

But Bentleigh Stringer's immediate enthusiasm for two of Danilov's manuscripts clinched the sale. Both titles were snapped up by Brayne-Watts, and Danilov was won over, even against his inner convictions.

At a subsequent meeting he explained to Stringer that he would have to operate from West Berlin because this was the only point where the underground could make contact now that Helsinki had been closed off. Danilov said he'd got himself a job with a printer in West Berlin.

Stringer and Danilov had formed a satisfactory and cordial working relationship, even though they had little in common and, in fact, secretly disliked each other. Bentleigh would be sure to say: 'Oh, Sheila sends her kindest regards and hopes one day to meet you,' or 'Sheila's opinion on this will be valuable. I'll leave it to her.' But Sheila never got to hear about it. As far as she was concerned it was Bentleigh who had opened up the Danilov contact through his own nerve and initiative, for which she continued to admire him.

Bentleigh had greatly enjoyed his monthly jaunts to West Berlin. To make them pay for themselves and to give a legitimate cover to the trips, tax-wise, he'd made an affiliation with a Berlin literary agent, Horst Baumgarten, and this had turned out reasonably well. Also, he'd met and enjoyed three Berlin girls, on the strength of which he'd taken back to London the opinion that 'Berlin girls not only let you. They help you.'

But not this evening. He had on his mind Horst Baumgarten's blonde secretary, Greta Ziegler. Her wide smiling blue-green eyes and her softly chiding voice had come into his mind intermittently on the plane. In fact, after the rendezvous with Danilov, he intended to ring her on the after-hours number she'd given him—to confirm his Monday appointment with her employer.

Bentleigh looked at his watch. It was two-thirty, almost an hour since Danilov had rung. Damn! There'd have been ample time to have had lunch at the hotel, and this really annoyed him. Most inconsiderate of Danilov. Two cars came into view and pulled in to the kerb across the street. A black DKW and a blue Volkswagen. The driver of the Volkswagen got out and had a few words with the driver of the DKW. Then he turned and walked down the lane.

8

Evans stood by the wall of the hut and watched the Volks-
Polizei stolidly checking passports and processing question-
naires down the line. Several paces from him a silent crowd
of people stood in an arc and watched. Some were Berliners
waiting for relatives to come through. They came here every
other day and waited for hours in the hope that someone they
knew would come through and give them news of the Eastern
Sector. And there were tourists—Americans, British, French,
Scandinavian. They stood silently and stared. Most of them
had come on the U-bahn. Just after two a 'Grosse Stadtrund-
fahrt' bus passed through packed with tourists on a three-
hour tour of East Berlin.

As a black BMW chugged across No Man's Land, an American left the hut and walked to the sandbag emplacement just
short of the white line that ran across the road. The BMW
crossed the white line. It was like making a touch-down. Or
one of those board-games with tokens you moved around:
'Do not pass go. Do not collect two hundred.'

One of the Americans was crouching behind the telescope in
the emplacement. Evans stepped into the hut and saw another
American put down his binoculars, take his black helmet from
a peg by the door and carefully adjust it on his head. He stepped
out onto the road. The major was on the phone at his desk.

The M.P. at the observation post was saying: 'Volkswagen at
the first control. Only one occupant. Male. Escorted into Vopo
hut for document check.'

Evans stared through the window of the checkpoint.

After a long time he said: 'There he is now.'

'Are you sure?' The major got up and joined him.

'I think so. It's a brown Renault.'

The major trained his binoculars on the Eastern checkpoint, trying to read the registration number.

'Four-two—seven, I think. There's snow on his bumper bar and it's hard to read.'

Evans turned away from the window. 'No. That's not Walkley. That's not his number.'

There was a long hold-up and Evans watched the front car. Behind the Renault a straggling queue of vehicles was piling up. Carbon monoxide from their exhausts curled upward and hung above the line of vehicles in a long snake of murky vapour. It was a bitterly cold afternoon.

Evans stepped out of the hut and lit his pipe and turned the bowl upside-down to protect the smouldering tobacco from the falling flecks of snow. He pulled up the collar of his gabardine overcoat and tugged at the brim of his hat. He was worried. And he was impatient. He'd been here several hours on and off since the M.P.'s phone call. After standing in the dark biting cold for four hours he'd gone back to the hotel for a shave, shower and breakfast. Then he'd come back and waited another four hours. It was now well after two o'clock, and there was still no sign of Walkley.

The Americans at the checkpoint had been as helpful as they could and seemed genuinely concerned. But though they'd started inquiries going in the proper channels no word had come through yet.

Evans waited for several more vehicles to come through. He was about to leave when he saw a brown Renault in the distance and his hopes rose. He went into the checkpoint and waited until the M.P. with the binoculars could read the numbers on the number-plate. It was not Walkley's.

He looked at his watch. Two-forty. He couldn't leave it any longer. He used the phone on the major's desk to call the

Hilton. He was told that Herr Stringer had arrived but that he had left the hotel. There was no message.

He checked with the major that nothing had come through about Walkley. Then he hurried out and caught a taxi to Schaperstrasse.

A man came hurrying up the lane, his shoulders hunched against the cold. He reached the Schaperstrasse and turned right, pressing close to the row of shops. Stringer straightened, loosening his shoulders and rehearsing the look of eager concern with which he would greet Danilov.

The figure had reached the mouth of the lane. A small hurrying shape in the inevitable grey-green duffel-coat. Danilov. There was no mistaking him.

As Stringer watched, the black DKW drove off.

Danilov came to the culvert. He was clutching something under his coat. He paused and looked both ways before stepping forward to cross the road. Fine snow was falling. The Russian looked a forlorn figure, more lonely, more furtive, perhaps, than usual. Or was Stringer imagining it? He turned and looked behind him, then pulled up the hood of his coat to cover his ears. With some semblance of a casual air he stepped out onto the road and made straight for the *pension*.

Just then he stiffened and stopped in his tracks. He jerked round sharply with shock. A brown paper parcel fell from the bottom of his duffel-coat onto the snow at his feet.

Bentleigh gave a gasp of horror.

Danilov clutched at his ribs. He crumpled and fell on his side. Bentleigh heard no shot or cry.

A man had come running from the lane. He stopped and grabbed the parcel, turned and ran to a blue Volkswagen that was parked nearby. He slid into the driver's seat, slammed the door and drove off.

Stringer stared at the misshapen grey-green smudge and saw the blood that had gushed from it to form a ragged shape on the snow-caked road.

Evans had seen it all as his taxi had pulled into Schaperstrasse. He ordered the driver to pull in to the kerb and got out quickly. A woman had come out of the delicatessen. Together they squatted at the Russian's side. She caught her breath several times as he examined Danilov. He was already dead. A bullet had entered his heart.

Evans said in German: 'Ring the police!'

The woman put a hand to her mouth and rushed back into the shop.

Evans rose and hurried to the taxi. 'Back to the checkpoint!'

The taxi drew up before the checkpoint and Evans paid him off. He stepped out and looked about him. It was still snowing lightly. There was a long queue of vehicles stacking up to go through the checkpoint.

The major was on the phone at the corner desk. When he saw Evans he waved him to a chair. Then he motioned to one of the M.P.s, who went into the annex and came out after a few seconds with a large mug of steaming coffee. He put it on the small table in front of Evans. Evans nodded his thanks.

He sat sipping the sweet hot liquid. It was too sweet, but Evans needed it. He groped for his pipe and pocket-knife. He opened out the small blade and began to scrape the bowl. After a time he emptied the scrapings into the grey steel waste-paper bin under the table.

'Huh-huh. Huh-huh.' The major was still listening. He nodded and made notes on a pad. Then he said: 'Thanks. I'll take it from here. Thank you.' He replaced the receiver and stood up. He came over to Evans.

'They've found your man Walkley.'

Evans looked up quickly then stood up.

The major said: 'He's been murdered.'

Evans looked at him. He looked down at the floor, then across at the observation window. 'Oh, Christ!' he muttered softly. Then he sat down and took a deep breath.

'West German and British M.P.s went across. They got permission to visit the morgue and found him.'

Evans didn't say anything. He pushed his coffee aside.

The American said: 'He was shot four times.'

'Were there any other marks on his body?'

'Yes. He'd been tortured.'

The M.P. at the window was saying: 'Skoda. Grey. Now at first checkpoint. Driver being escorted into Vopo hut.'

The major said: 'Do you know anyone named Schmidt?'

Evans turned. 'Schmidt?'

'Jonas Schmidt.'

Evans nodded. 'There was a Jonas. Walkley was going to meet him at the opera.'

'He was tortured and killed too. He was in the morgue with Walkley.' After a pause he said: 'The British police have recovered Walkley's Renault. It's at the British M.P. command post.'

9

Bentleigh Stringer entered his suite and locked the door. He made for the bureau and poured himself a Scotch. Then he began to pace the thick carpet and talk to himself, pausing at each turn to look at himself in the large wall-mirrors.

Was this the end of the golden eggs? The thought appalled him. First Nubrov. Now Danilov.

Occasionally, Bentleigh raised a small be-ringed and well-manicured hand to remove his cigar and blow out a stream of smoke in a slightly impatient gesture, conscious only of Bentleigh Stringer. Bentleigh was always conscious of himself, an admiring bystander observing the inexhaustible quirks and qualities of Bentleigh Stringer. Bentleigh Stringer being a gentleman. Bentleigh Stringer being sincere. Bentleigh Stringer being a bastard. It was a subject that never ceased to fascinate him. He would have liked to see himself stricken by the Russian's death. But it didn't sit too well on his rounded pink face. So he admitted quite honestly that he'd never really cared for Danilov. He'd found the Russian's intense idealism embarrassing. Bentleigh always felt a little uncomfortable when confronted with selfless service to a cause, particularly a lost cause.

The big question was: Shouldn't he think of his own skin now and catch the next plane back to London? He paced the room and caught up with his reflection again and thought he saw his brother-in-law nodding wisely. Write it off. Get out. Rest on your laurels. This underground thing couldn't have gone on for ever anyway. Catch the next plane to London where there is less chance of being shot down in the street.

He went to the telephone and put his hand on the receiver. Wait!

Was this really the end? Did it have to be? The underground knew he was staying here at the Hilton. With Danilov dead, wouldn't they conceivably try to contact him? A fresh contact to replace Danilov? Or would they start trying to contact Sheila again? In the mirror he could see Sheila regarding him with heavy-lidded contempt.

The phone rang under his hand.

He raised the receiver. 'Yes?'

'Herr Stringer?' It was a soft low female voice.

'Yes.'

'Ah!' There was pleasure in the sound. 'This is Greta Ziegler. Herr Baumgarten's secretary.'

Stringer straightened, caught by surprise. The provocative lilt of her voice conjured a picture of a smiling mouth with a short upper lip and large blue-green eyes that mocked him.

'Yes, Fräulein!'

She said: 'I was just checking that your appointment with Herr Baumgarten was all right for ten o'clock in the morning.'

'Certainly, Fräulein Ziegler. And thank you for thinking of me on a Sunday afternoon. It is *most* thoughtful of you!'

She gave a little laugh. 'Well, I was sitting here and thinking of you arriving in Berlin today. It is such a lonely city if you do not know anyone!'

He invited her to dinner. When she hesitated he began to mention some of West Berlin's most lavish restaurants. There was a silence when he'd run out of suggestions. He thought of the pause as of a penny standing on its edge wondering which way to fall.

'Herr Stringer, I wonder if you'd mind——' His heart sank. It sounded like a refusal. But she said: 'I wonder if you'd mind eating at *my* place? It will be quieter here and the conversation will be *much* pleasanter than at a restaurant.'

Bentleigh accepted instantly. She gave him an address in Schöneberg. The time, eight o'clock. He hung up. With a beaming smile of anticipation he saw the penny fall heads up.

It was 3.50 p.m. by the time Evans reached Wilmersdorf. He found the address Walkley had given him. It was a new apartment building with a well-kept garden. He went upstairs into the lobby and sought the *concierge*. A plump business-like woman came out. He said he was a friend of Herr Walkley and wanted to see his room.

She said stonily: 'Herr Walkley is not in. And he did not come home last night.'

He nodded. 'Fräulein, this is a matter of life and death. It may be a matter for the British police. I want to see Herr Walkley's apartment.'

After a moment's hesitation she stepped into her small office and got a key. 'Come.' He followed her up the stairs.

She opened the door and went in. Evans followed.

The woman uttered an exclamation. The small apartment was in a mess. There were papers strewn about the floor. The cushions had been slashed open and kapok spread over the divan. His two suitcases had been forced open.

Evans looked around the room. He stooped and picked up a sheet of paper from the floor. He read the scrawling handwriting:

> The crowd of cripples at the gate
> Turned their faces to the east
> Away from the morning smell of charcoal
> And wept their fill.

He folded the sheet and put it in his pocket. He said: 'Leave everything as it is. I will inform the British police.'

He hurried downstairs and left the building.

10

Bentleigh Stringer was at the door of the apartment in Schöneberg. Standing erect, his heavy top-coat over his arm, he pressed the buzzer. The door opened and he saw the girl.

She was standing before him in a pale-green sleeveless sheath. It made her fair skin and Nordic high-cheek-boned face look cool and lovely. Her shoulders were somehow set for something special, and the way her hips were slightly turned to one side in the sheath made him feel as young as his steambath had made him look. And she seemed pleasantly startled at his appearance as she extended her hand.

'Herr Stringer. And on the stroke of eight!' Her voice was a warm caress. So was her hand.

Those first few moments set the mood. All was elegance and sophistication. The luxurious apartment was as spacious as a palace. The music from the record-player was Brahms, just within earshot. As she served the Martinis it seemed to Bentleigh that her admiring glances, the faint brushing of her shoulder against his lapel were accidental, but they were firm enough for him to think that they were surreptitious. The preliminary conversation went smoothly. They were both experts of the cocktail hour.

'Such an expensive apartment for a working girl,' he murmured with an amused but pointed sweep of the arm.

'My papa makes beer,' she explained. 'Very good beer—in Munich.'

'I see.' He turned to face her, smiling. 'So you don't *have* to work.'

'Not to exist. Only to live.'

She talked with spontaneous enthusiasm and sometimes a quick flash of humour. She mentioned Herr Baumgarten, and Baumgarten's clients, most of whom she regarded as stodgy. She envied Bentleigh his freedom on the choice of authors and titles, his derring-do, his fresh courageous outlook. And she openly wished that she could do something similar. When Stringer showed cautious interest in this remark she said:

'But Herr Baumgarten won't even *look* at such a manuscript.' She shrugged regretfully. 'He says it is too dangerous —that we must not get involved with the underground or politics. How can anyone write today if they don't want to get involved in politics? *Old* people like Herr Baumgarten don't want to get involved.'

The words hung pleasantly between them. Then she took his empty glass and strolled across to the cocktail bar and made two fresh Martinis.

Presently, there was a buzz at the door and Greta went to answer it. A waiter entered silently and crossed into the dining-room wheeling a trolley laden with hot steel trays and covers. As soon as he'd left, closing the door silently behind him, she led Bentleigh into the dining-room.

During the meal Greta drew him out and made him tell her about himself. He spoke with boyish enthusiasm, being careful not to mention Sheila. He spoke grandly of his break-through—how he was contacted first in Helsinki by a young Russian translator named Nubrov, how he'd taken a chance and brought the manuscript back to Britain. The immediate break-through with the sale of *Tyrants*. He told it with gusto and unscrupulous dishonesty. His words tumbled over themselves and his face beamed with triumph as he told it.

Once, when Greta asked about his partner, Sheila Swann—Was that her name?—he replied vaguely: 'Oh, Sheila takes care of the New York office. I really don't see much of her.'

Over liqueurs Greta sighed, with a deep shrug of her lovely shoulders. 'If only I could get Herr Baumgarten to be so adventurous! Not even when I come across a sensational underground manuscript does he show any interest!'

Bentleigh didn't rise to the bait. He wanted to stay off business for this evening. Maybe she had something to sell. Maybe she didn't. It was time he took over.

He rose and went to the cocktail bar and brought the Cointreau bottle to the table. He refilled her glass then stood behind her chair and put the bottle aside. He put his hands on her shoulders and said: 'What a lovely neck you have.'

He felt her soft skin tense, then relax. She turned, slid up out of her chair and came into his arms. He found her lips. They were warm and soft.

He found kissing her unusually exciting, and he was thinking, hell, that was easy. The Turkish bath had done the job, put an edge on his charm. He felt he could handle it. She was sophisticated and well-bred. She was no schoolgirl and she was European. Europeans didn't waste time on preliminaries. After several more kisses he made a reluctant gesture to sit down and finish their liqueurs. She shook her head.

'I shall bring them upstairs,' she said softly.

He nodded and left her.

When he came back from the toilet the trolley had gone and the candles on the table were out. The record-player was playing a soft Mancini. He stole upstairs to where a shaft of light flooded the landing. He reached the top, turned right and went silently along the thickly carpeted landing and came to an open door. He looked in and found a large bedroom. It was luxuriously furnished, the largest item being the canopied double bed. The room was bathed in a pink glow from the ruffled silk bedside lamp. There was a long body under the single sheet. A bundle of fair hair was spread out on the pillow. Lower down, the breasts stood out in two mounds, caressed by the pink glow from the shaded lamp. Two filled

65

liqueur glasses stood on the bedside table, the half-empty bottle beside them.

Bentleigh Stringer stood stockstill at the sight of her. He gave a short involuntary chuckle. Then he came forward and tweaked her nose. She gave a little squeal of protest. In less than a minute he was under the sheet beside her.

He kissed her tenderly, tentatively. He slid his hand onto her left breast, then to her hip, then to the warmth and down. Her arms went round him and he felt a surge of excitement induced by desire and grounded in conquest. For the first time since the early days of Sheila, every cliché about the physical impact of sudden desire became true for him. He felt an un-inhibited response from her lithe young body. Her legs shifted to his demands and she moaned softly and made little crooning noises.

When it was over and peace came he knew that nothing could be the same again for them. Craftily, he thought of Sheila, then of Dorothy. Then he thought of Baumgarten. There had been a subtle shift in meanings, in associations. And something had been started. He had altered his direction. He knew it was a dangerous direction. He thought of Danilov and saw him lying on the white road, all the intensity and idealism draining from him into the red blot on the snow.

After a time, they lit up cigarettes and talked quietly and made jokes. Now and then she gave a little gurgling laugh. Greta said what about their liqueurs and he turned over and half sat up and got them. It was a nice time.

'What a team we'd make,' he murmured.

She gave a luxurious wriggle. 'I have always thought so.'

He looked at her curiously. 'You have?'

The tips of her fingers showed, the nails long, polished with silver, holding the sheet up to her neck. Her large blue-green eyes inspected him. She nodded.

'I have thought about you a lot, Bentleigh darling.' After a little she added: 'I admire you—and what you stand for.'

He could have made a ribald comment about that, but he

nodded appreciatively. 'Sensible girl. With brains too!' He said airily, as though he'd just thought of it: 'I'd like you to come into business with me—say, in Paris or somewhere.'

She sat up, still holding the sheet. 'You would?'

He studied her. Was her surprise genuine? He couldn't tell. He said off-handedly: 'You'd be interested?'

She lay back. After a thoughtful pause she said: 'Let us say —it is worth thinking about.'

There was another long pause. Then she suddenly turned from him, leaned over and opened the drawer of the bedside table. She took from it a large envelope. She handed it to him.

'Maybe this could be our first title.'

His mouth fell open. He looked at the blank envelope, then at her. 'You bitch!' he muttered with a laugh. 'What do you know?' He chuckled again, highly amused. 'Greta Ziegler is a trick!'

He slid the manuscript from the envelope. It was quite slim, no more than thirty-odd pages, stapled together at the top left-hand corner.

'Is this all there is?'

'That's the first chapter.'

'I see. The carrot?'

She nodded. 'Something like that. Excuse me.' She slid out of bed and put on her wrap and went silently to the bathroom.

Left alone, Bentleigh lit a cigar and then looked at the title page. It read:

The Making of Korablov
by Anatoly Marakov

The title meant nothing to Stringer. He didn't know who Korablov was, though the name sounded vaguely familiar. He began to read:

Before there is a corpse, there is always a *zapiska*. That is the way things are done in Smersh. Smersh means 'Smiert Spionam'—

'Death to Spies'—and its headquarters are at Number 13 Srelenka Ulista, Moscow. It operates throughout the Soviet Union, and, in fact, in every country in the world, and employs more than forty thousand men and women.

Like all administrations, there has to be a system, a production line. Rather like a printing office, in Smersh each job begins with a Job File. The Job File has a shiny black cover. A thick white stripe runs diagonally across it from top-right to bottom-left. In the top right-hand space there are the letters SS in white, then 'Sovershennoe Sekretno', the equivalent to 'Top Secret'. Across the centre is neatly printed in white letters the name of the job. The file is called a *zapiska*.

When the head of the KGB wants someone killed, he first rings through to Central Index at Smersh on the closed-circuit telephone and asks: 'Have you a *zapiska* on——' and states the name of the potential victim.

It is very much to Smersh's credit if there is already a *zapiska* on this enemy of the Soviet Republic.

That is why there is a large staff of researchers at Srenlenka Ulitsa who do nothing else but look for enemies of the State and create *zapiskas* for spies, writers, aviators, football players and dustmen. They read through sheaves of press-clippings that flood in from the Russian Embassies around the world, and from these they pick out those who merit a *zapiska*.

I am telling you all this for two reasons. One, because I want you to believe what I am telling you, and, two, because it will help you to understand how the Korablov thing began.

Well, it began on November 3, 1955, when a *zapiska* was created for an English spy.

I remember that across the centre of this file was neatly printed in white letters:

COMMANDER LIONEL CRABB, ENGLISH SPY

Bentleigh Stringer sat up. He shot a quick look toward the bathroom door. Then he stared back at the typewritten page. *The Crabb Affair!*

68

11

Some time after ten, Evans went back to the Europa and rang room service and had them send up a plate of lobster sandwiches and a bottle of Scotch. He sat on the bed and thought about the mess. First Hannifin. Now Walkley. Hannifin defected, Walkley dead. Tortured first, then murdered. Danilov dead. Jonas Schmidt dead. The underground pipe-line cut off. The whole Berlin operation in a shambles. Now what? What do you do now? Start again? Start where?

He munched a sandwich and washed it down with Scotch and water and thought: I should have stopped Walkley. I should have pulled him out and sent him back to London for further training. Training for what? For survival? Then he thought: Training wouldn't matter. We were all just as vulnerable. It's the bloody world we live in. There's no answer to a shot in the dark or a stab in the back. We've got to live with these terrors for just as long as we can, like an infantryman in the firing line. Nobody's smarter than anyone else.

Evans poured himself a glass of neat Scotch and drank it down straight. There's nothing else. We just go on like this, clinging to what we know, to our friends if we have any, to our love if we have one, to our tradition if it means anything any more. Otherwise there is nothing. We finish up like this, in a hotel room with a bottle of whisky, knowing nothing and loving nothing.

The phone rang. He looked at it and let it ring. After several seconds it rang again. He got up and answered it.

'Hallo.' His voice was scarcely audible. There was no edge to it.

'What are you doing?' He recognized Sara's voice. It sounded soft and kind. He wanted to hang up.

He said: 'Getting tight.'

'May I come over and get tight with you?'

'No.'

'I'm coming anyway.'

'Suit yourself.'

'I'll come and bring a bottle.'

'It's a free country.'

'There's something you should know about me, Evans.'

'What's that?'

'I'm hard to get.'

'So.'

'All you've got to do is ask me.'

She hung up.

He put back the receiver, slightly annoyed with himself for letting her bully him. He went to the door and clipped back the bolt. Then he put the whisky bottle and the plate of sandwiches on the floor. He sat on the carpet near them, his back leaning against the bed.

He poured himself another drink and broke it down to half-strength with water. The one solid shot was enough to set him up. Now he wanted to drift, neither down nor up. Straight ahead. A planter's punch. He thought of Danilov and saw him shot down on the road. But what did it matter? What did anything matter? What was left for anyone in this precarious, impossible balance between right and wrong, Right and Left, black and white? What was left but to try to go on, to try to make your voice heard, a voice that would try to make partial order out of total chaos? This was what the Soviet underground writers were trying to do. They were trying to be heard, trying to publish, trying to tell the world about the terrors of totalitarianism, trying to warn it. They were saying to other writers: Be yourself while you can. Every individual must try to be himself. If he relinquishes this privilege he ceases to be a human being. He ceases to be free.

The door opened and Sara came in. She was wearing her Betty Boops and a big fur coat and a fur hat and gloves. She looked like a space-child. She was holding a long package which she stood up on the dressing-table.

'Well, well, Evans! You're making quite a picnic of it!'

When he didn't reply she took off her coat, hat and gloves and put them on the upholstered chair by the window. She came and stood by him, looking down. She looked about fifteen.

'Is this a private war or can anyone join in?'

When he didn't reply she sat on the floor beside him and poured a drink. She leaned against him slightly.

'You'd rather I shut up, wouldn't you?'

He nodded.

She said gently: 'All right, Evans. I don't know what's hit you. But whatever it is, I'd like it to hit me, too. Just a little of it.'

They sat in silence and drank, and they cleaned off the lobster sandwiches.

After a long time he said:

'He was interested in you.'

'Who?'

'Walkley.'

'Who's Walkley?'

'A man,' Evans said. 'He'd have suited you too.'

'Why?'

'He was nearer your age.'

After a pause, she said: 'Interested in me? Whenever did he see me?'

'At the airport.'

'The airport? I didn't see anybody there.'

'He was shy. Didn't like to interrupt our affair.'

There was another long silence. Sara refilled their glasses.

She asked: 'Where is he now?'

'Who?'

'Walkley.'

'Dead.' After a long time he said: 'They tortured him first. Then they shot him four times.'

They sat in silence and drank.

When Stringer returned to the Hilton he was still dazed by his good fortune and exhilarated by the other triumphs of the evening. Now in the sumptuous privacy of the hotel suite he permitted his true emotions full reign. He lit a fresh cigar and opened up a bottle of cold champagne, poured himself a glass and paced the carpet. He thought excitedly of the manuscript. My God, if the rest of the manuscript lives up to the sample! He had taken the script from its envelope and thrown it onto the bedspread where he could keep it in sight. The Crabb Affair. That was the name the newspapers had given it. Biennially and on the slightest provocation they rehashed the gruesome, if meagre, details of the circumstances in which Commander Lionel Phillip Kenneth Crabb met his death.

An avid reader of London's newspapers, Bentleigh knew almost by heart the details of the distorted undersea saga that had captured the imagination of twenty million readers. He knew that a book purporting to be the final word—the indisputable and incontrovertible truth—on the fate of Commander Crabb would be a sensation.

Now he stopped and faced his summing up with excitement, glad he was alone to savour it, glad he had time to spare without anyone to badger him with ideas and red herrings. He picked up the script now and paced with it, tapping it across his wrist. It was potentially the greatest publishing scoop of the decade. It was in a way overdue, as unstoppable as an idea about to happen. He hadn't told Greta any of this. In fact, he'd scarcely revealed any interest in it, as a matter of business.

He recalled with a chuckle how his cigar had fallen from his mouth and how he'd bounded out of bed beating the burning ash off his stomach. He'd got back into bed and was poised and thoughtful when she came back from the bathroom and rejoined him. They'd discussed the manuscript airily on a 'what if it's good' basis. But for the time being, he'd told her, you'll have to trust me. I'll have to take the manuscript back to London and read it carefully to satisfy myself that it is genuine. This might take a week, perhaps longer. She'd have to trust him. Meanwhile there were some things he wanted to know.

'How did you come by this manuscript?' he asked.

'I have a friend at the university. He is studying philosophy. He knew I was a literary agent and brought it to me to look at.'

'Did you tell Herr Baumgarten?'

'No. I had already sounded him out on the subject and he did not want to discuss it. Besides, I knew *you* would be over soon.'

'Good girl. Now, what are the conditions of sale?'

'Anatoly Marakov is sick. He needs money.'

'How much?'

'Ten thousand pounds sterling, paid into a bank in Switzerland in his name. His signature is appended on the title page.'

'So I noticed.' He put the manuscript aside and turned to her. 'You'll have to trust me, my love.'

To prove that she understood and that he was genuine, they made love again, this time light-heartedly, as the sharers of a new-found secret that would bring them excitement and wealth together.

Afterwards, he went into the bathroom, then returned and began to dress.

She said: 'Must you leave so early?'

'I must, my dear.'

She put on a wrap and came downstairs with him. In the hall she helped him on with his topcoat. At the door she clung to him lingeringly, then pushed him away with a reluctant sigh.

'Next time I shall have more time,' he promised.

He turned and strode along the carpeted corridor.

Now he sat on the bed in his suite with the manuscript on his

73

knee. He re-read it. Then he sat for a long time, drinking champagne and thinking. What incredible luck. When one door shuts another opens. Today the underground's pipeline was cut. This evening, only hours later, a new one had been opened.

He thought of Anatoly Marakov. He looked again at the title page and examined the signature. He wondered about Marakov's standing in the Soviet Union. *The Making of Korablov*. Was this the truth? Bentleigh knew that before he could submit this first chapter to Brayne-Watts he would have to have it checked. He put the manuscript aside and began to pace again, puffing furiously at his cigar. Check him out. Check him out. He stopped. His brother-in-law, Christopher West. Naval Intelligence. Yes. Chris could check the manuscript and tell him if it was genuine. He paced again. Would Chris be appalled by it, whether it were true or false? Yes. Probably would. He'd try to dissuade Bentleigh from handling it or having anything to do with it. After all, it was showing the SIS up in a very poor light.

Bentleigh stopped again. The SIS. Evans. Michael Evans. He was the man. The very man to check the manuscript. Pay him enough money and he'd have no scruples about the SIS. And he knew more of the inside details of the Secret Service than Chris did anyhow. *And* the KGB, and before it, the MVD. And Evans was in Berlin right now, staying at the Europa.

Bentleigh crossed to the phone. He hesitated, looking at his watch. It was three-ten. Pretty late to ring someone and talk business. Well, he was paying for it. He picked up the phone and asked the night clerk to put him through to the Europa.

Sara had removed her spectacles. Now she had her knees hunched up under her and her head was on Evans's lap. His hand rested on the back of her neck. He thought she was like an affectionate kitten or a faithful puppy. She stayed like that for a long time.

The phone rang, one sharp sudden ring. He looked up at it helplessly and she stirred.

It rang again and she scrambled up and crossed over Evans in her stocking feet. She picked up the receiver and passed it down to him.

'Hallo.'

'Michael Evans?'

'Yes.'

'Bentleigh Stringer.'

Evans sat forward. He hadn't thought of Stringer since Danilov's death. 'Yes?'

'I'm about to check out and fly back to London. Any chance of seeing you before I leave?'

Evans hesitated, looking at Sara. 'Well, Bentleigh, it's pretty late——'

'I know. I'm sorry. But a very important matter has come up, Michael. Can I call round at your hotel on the way to the airport?'

Sara was sitting on the bed, pulling on her knee-boots.

Evans said: 'Well, okay.'

'You'll be alone?'

'Yes.'

'Thank you.' The line went dead.

Evans replaced the receiver and got up. 'My agent. He's dropping in to see me. Something important.'

'That's all right, Evans.' She was putting on her hat. 'Thanks for the nicest drink-in I've ever had.' She gave him a wide smile.

He went and got her coat and helped her into it.

'Something important apparently. He's calling in on the way to the airport.' He picked up the package from the dressing-table. 'Here. Don't leave this.'

She made him put it back. 'Nonsense, Evans. Leave it here. It'll be an excuse to invite me over for another drink-in.'

He stood uncertainly, looking at her. She crinkled her nose and smiled up at him, then stood on tip-toe and kissed him.

'Thanks,' he said.

She went to the door, blew him a kiss and left the room silently, closing the door after her.

Evans stripped off and went into the bathroom. He got under the hot shower and stood there for a good five minutes. Then he turned on the cold water for ten seconds. He came out into the bedroom and quickly dried himself, then he got into his pyjamas.

There was a knock on the door. He opened it and let Stringer in. Stringer was in his topcoat and carrying a large brown envelope. Evans hated him for his beaming expectant smile and for not looking the slightest bit put out over Danilov.

'Hope you don't mind,' the agent said. 'But I'm on my way to the airport. I have a taxi waiting below.'

Evans nodded. He could smell a woman's scent all over Stringer, cloying and unsubtle.

Bentleigh put on a sober look. 'I've had a shocking day, really. This afternoon I saw a man murdered—right before my eyes.'

Evans nodded. 'Danilov. I was there.'

'What?' Stringer stared at Evans in amazement. 'You—but how——?'

'I was in a taxi. I saw him shot down by the man in the blue Volkswagen.'

Stringer was speechless. He remembered the man in the gabardine coat squatting beside the body with the woman.

'It was a dreadful thing!'

After a pause of several seconds he slipped the manuscript from the envelope.

'I——' he hesitated sheepishly. 'I wanted to see you about this. It's very important.'

'What is it?'

'An underground manuscript. In fact, it's only the first chapter, but——'

'I don't understand. Danilov failed to make contact with you. Where did you get this?'

'Another contact.'

'From the underground?'

'Yes. A—a—person I've known for some time contacted me. When I went to see her she gave me this.' He handed Evans the manuscript.

Evans read the title page. There was a pause. Stringer stood awkwardly and looked at his wristwatch.

Evans said: 'The Making of Korablov.' He looked quickly at Stringer. 'Korablov? Lvev Lvovich Korablov?'

'Lionel Crabb.'

Evans turned to the opening page of the narrative and began to read the first paragraph.

Stringer said: 'Look. I must go. Can I leave this script with you? Will you read it and tell me whether you think it's genuine?'

'I'd be keen to.'

The agent looked vastly relieved. 'Now, if you'll permit me, I'd like to discuss a fee——'

'What for?'

'For vetting the manuscript. And a foreword, say, a thousand words, as an ex-member of MI5——'

Evans looked at him and thought: You cunning bastard.

Bentleigh went on: 'Say, five per cent of the author's royalty. How does that sound?'

'I'll read it first, then I'll let you know.'

'Splendid. That's it, then.' He looked quickly at his watch. 'I must go.'

He shook Evans's hand. Evans opened the door for him and said: 'I'll give you a ring.'

'Thanks, if you would.'

Evans closed the door after him.

12

Evans knew a lot about the Crabb affair. A fairly new recruit to intelligence work, he'd been in London at the time and knew it as a bitter memory for the SIS, even though he'd not been personally involved. More than any other incident, with the possible exception of Philby's double game, it had gone down in history as the greatest gaffe put up by the British Secret Service since the war.

The sensational incident occurred in 1956 during a ten-day State visit by the Soviet Prime Minister, Marshal Bulganin, and the head of the Russian Communist Party, Nikita Krushchev. They had travelled to England aboard the cruiser *Ordzhonikidze*, escorted by two destroyers, *Sovershenny* and *Smotryashchi*. The three ships docked at Portsmouth. All seemed to be going well with the visit when Mr Krushchev made a remark at a press conference about certain 'sharp moments' and 'under-water rocks'—a remark which had completely mystified the British Prime Minister.

Evans remembered the two days of panic and consternation that had followed; then the disclosure that Commander Crabb, a former R.N.V.R. officer and experienced frogman, was missing presumed dead as a result of an 'accident' during trials with under-water apparatus near Portsmouth Harbour; and fourteen months later, the headless, handless body of a diver being found near Pilsey Island in Chichester Harbour; the inquest a few weeks later and the finding that the body was that of Crabb.

Since Crabb's mysterious disappearance the British press had published many fantastic and macabre 'think-pieces' about the British wartime hero. Evans had read weird stories featuring sinister agents of the MVD, and bumbling officers of the British Secret Intelligence Service. They were always good for a laugh: 'Crabb had been killed by an anti-frogman device attached to the hull of the *Ordzhonikidze*.' He had been trapped 'in a television cable as he filmed the hull of the cruiser'. 'Emissions, directed at him from an asdic dome under the *Smotryashchi*' had caused his instant death. He was protecting the Russian ships 'from the actions of a fanatical Right-wing émigré group who planned to assassinate the Russian leaders by attaching a limpet mine to the cruiser'. 'Crabb had discovered the mine just in time and removed it from the hull and was carrying it to a safe distance away from the ship when it had exploded.' And then there was the version in which Crabb had been captured by waiting Russian frogmen and taken back to Russia in the sickbay of the *Ordzhonikidze*. 'He was given the choice of being shot as a spy,' one article had recounted, 'or of joining the Soviet Navy— on condition that he was never asked to spy on British ships. This condition was accepted, and Crabb joined the Russian Navy under the name of Lvev Lvovich Korablov.'

Before reading the manuscript, Evans thought about it carefully. It had come mysteriously into Stringer's hands only a few hours after the death of Danilov, Walkley and Schmidt— after the underground's 'official' pipeline had been cut. Yet this did not prove anything. It still could be genuine. Many writers behind the Iron Curtain would be able to get their manuscripts through to the West. He began to read.

Following the brief opening, Evans read:

At that time I was employed as a translator in the Smersh Central Index.

I am telling you this, even though I know that the instant this manuscript is seen by Smersh, orders will be given for a *zapiska* to be created for me—Anatoly Marakov—wherever I happen to be at the time.

And whereas thousands of other *zapiskas* may lie dormant for years before being acted upon or going into the archives, mine will be sent to the head of the KGB, who will rubber-stamp it for urgent action. The rubber-stamp will be in red. Immediately below my name, it will read:

KILL.

Sometimes it happens the other way round. Sometimes the head of the KGB wants to implement some action to intimidate a foreign power or to create a situation. He will call for a group of *zapiskas* and read them carefully, then pick one out and overstamp it in red with the dreaded word.

Or, he may call for a file and withdraw it from Smersh altogether.

This is what happened with the original *zapiska* on Commander Lionel Crabb.

I remember that the *zapiska* was originated on the order of the then head of Smersh, Colonel-General Radviliski. To the short written order was attached a clipping from the London *Times*. It showed a wartime picture of a small spare man who looked rather like a jockey. He was Commander Lionel Phillip Kenneth Crabb, a British war-hero. No reason was given in the General's request for a secret file to be created for him, and I read the press clipping with only a vague interest.

But a few days later I saw the reason for the *zapiska*.

An MVD agent in Britain had sent through a report stating that Commander Crabb had made an underwater investigation of the bottom of the Russian cruiser *Sverdlov*, as it lay at anchor in Portsmouth Harbour during a visit to Britain a few weeks previously in October 1955.

I added this report to the *zapiska* and moved it from 'Information Only' to 'Hold', for I had the feeling that it would soon be called in for action.

But here I must depart from my personal narrative and piece together the sequence of events as they actually happened. I emphasize that I have seen all the documents mentioned and have listened to the play-back of the recorded discussions, for they were later sent to the archives for permanent storage.

The date is January 10, 1956, the time 1100 hours.

General Dmitrov, Chief of the Committee of the Soviet State Security (MVD) received a top-secret memorandum that had been passed to him directly from the Soviet Prime Minister, Marshal Bulganin, for 'eyes only' examination and recommendation.

As soon as Dmitrov saw that the file had been originated by Captain Ivan Strelchuk, chief of the Special Task Underwater Operational Command at Sevastopol, he was immediately interested, for he'd had occasion to call on Strelchuk's frogmen for many sabotage and reconnaissance missions.

Strelchuk's document covered the history of the development of underwater strategic techniques and training methods during and since World War Two. It listed the number of surface vessels and installations that had been destroyed by Soviet divers, and referred to several of the more audacious exploits which had been carried out by courageous divers of both sides. It led through carefully documented steps to the present and projected expansion programmes of the Soviet submarine fleet, in which the requirement for underwater personnel had been exploded far beyond previously forecast figures.

The plain fact was that the value of the underwater arm had suddenly been recognized by all branches of the Navy and Army and that the numbers required urgently had put an impossible strain on the Underwater Operational Command's training establishment.

'There is an immediate requirement for key trainers with skill, courage and experience and a knowledge of modern underwater instruments and defensive and offensive weapons. The Soviet Union just does not have these people.'

The document urged that recruitment of training experts should go beyond the borders of the Soviet Union and Warsaw Pact countries.

'There are experienced, courageous and dedicated divers in Britain, France, Italy and the United States. While it would be too much of a risk to accept a defector from America, it is believed that in the other countries mentioned there are divers of great experience who might be induced to come to the Soviet Union to put into practice their pet theories and be able to carry on their diving careers not only unhampered by lack of finance but considerably aided by the most modern equipment.

'There are, perhaps, half a dozen men in the world who would be of inestimable value to our underwater training programme, and whose recruitment would save a year or more of trial-and-error experiment. These men are intrepid, even fanatical, underwater operators whose first loyalty is to the fascinating underwater world they have discovered.

'Could this matter be looked into?'

Dmitrov read the names of the people Strelchuk wanted to recruit. On top of the list was:

BRITAIN: Commander Lionel Crabb.

General Dmitrov picked up the receiver of a telephone marked in white with the letters *Vch*. These letters stood for *vysokochastoty*, or high frequency. Only some fifty supreme officials are connected to the Vch switchboard. He dialled a single number and waited while the phone rang, anticipating the crisp tense voice of the Colonel-General Radviliski.

'Yes.' The head of Smersh came on the line.

'Dmitrov speaking. Note this name carefully, Comrade. Commander Lionel Crabb. British. Do you have a *zapiska* for this man?'

'One moment, Comrade General.'

The MVD Chief waited. He visualized the Smersh chief picking up the receiver of another telephone, the 'Commandant' Telephone of the MVD. All lines were direct. There was no central switchboard.

Radviliski dialled a number.

It was I—Anatoly Marakov—who answered. 'Yes, Comrade General.'

'Central Index? The *zapiska* of Commander Lionel Crabb, ex-British Navy. Emergency. At once, Comrade.'

'Yes, Comrade General.'

Radviliski replaced the receiver.

Dmitrov said: 'You have already a *zapiska* on Crabb?'

'We have, Comrade General. And we have classified him as a dangerous enemy of the State, for he has recently executed hazardous work for the British Navy and the British Secret Service. He is therefore a spy from whom no Russian ship in British waters can be considered safe. We have listed him for possible liquidation.'

'Very interesting.'

There was a pause. Small-talk on the Vch line is avoided. A slip of the tongue, a clumsy choice of words can be highly dangerous.

The recorded conversations are often replayed in the light of changing situations and alliances.

The Smersh chief was sitting erect in his high-backed chair, waiting for the file to come through. On the walls of his office were a portrait of Stalin over the door, one of Lenin between the two windows; portraits of Bulganin and Krushchev; and where until January 13th, 1954, a portrait of Beria had hung, was a portrait of Dmitrov himself.

Evans read these details and thought: These unnecessary facts are for MI5—to prove the authenticity of Marakov's story. He would know that at least one MI5 man had seen the inside of this office. He read on:

The internal office telephone purred softly. General Radviliski lifted the receiver, listened briefly and said: 'Send it in.'

I knocked on the door, then entered the office carrying the Crabb *zapiska*. I put it on the desk in front of the General.

He spoke on the Vch phone: 'I have the *zapiska* in front of me, Comrade General. Commander Lionel Crabb. English Spy.'

Dmitrov said: 'That is the man.'

'We have a complete dossier on his mission under the *Sverdlov*. Do you want me to send it forward for Smiert-Action?'

'No, Comrade. Send it safe-hand to me for the time being. You may possibly lose this man to Defect-Action.'

'Very well, Comrade General.'

Radviliski hung up, slightly deflated. He hated to lose a *zapiska*— a potential result which would fill a space in his gold-engraved volumes.

It was not until the following afternoon that General Dmitrov was able to find time to examine the Crabb file. In addition to the dossier on the *Sverdlov* mission it now contained several newspaper and magazine clippings supplied by the Russian Embassy in London. The man was apparently thought of highly in Britain. Now a civilian, he was often hired by the Royal Navy for underwater jobs such as testing new equipment.

The dossier contained a reconstruction of the *Sverdlov* job by a British MVD operative, Number 219, whom Dmitrov knew to be a man named Rawlins. It described how Crabb and an SIS officer had hired a caravan at Southsea and used it as their base. How Crabb had bought a new black Pirelli dry-suit. How he'd made the dive at first light. Rawlins concluded that the whole operation was a waste of time. The only value from it was that he had confirmed that there were no secret fittings of any kind on the bottom of the *Sverdlov*'s hull.

Rawlins reported that he had struck up a close attachment with Crabb. Crabb, a poor security risk, talked in his cups. He had actually told Rawlins that the purpose of the scrutiny had been to find out if the *Sverdlov*'s lower hull was fitted with hatches for dropping nuclear mines!

Dmitrov grinned over this. '*Y'b nna mat!*' he muttered.

The British couldn't have been further from the truth. For although nuclear mines were a frightening possibility which had not been overlooked by the Presidium, Soviet nuclear scientists and aerodynamics experts were concentrating all their efforts on ICBMs and space satellites. But the information was slotted away for future reference.

That afternoon a communication was despatched from the MVD per medium of the diplomatic valise to the Soviet Embassy in London. It contained two messages, both to be delivered by dead-drop. One was to Rawlins. The other was to Number 115, an agent who worked for the MVD, operating inside MI5.

The first note, which reached Rawlins the following evening, instructed Rawlins to keep Crabb under surveillance.

The second instructed 115 to watch for any future mission involving the use of underwater personnel, and in particular, employing Commander Crabb.

On February 8, at a meeting with the Soviet Prime Minister, Marshal Bulganin, and the head of the Communist Party, Nikita Krushchev, General Dmitrov was informed that the two leaders had accepted an invitation by the British Prime Minister, Sir Anthony Eden, to visit Britain for the purpose of discussing trade between the two countries. Dmitrov knew that many months of careful planning and diplomatic discussion had already gone into this decision. The forthcoming visit was due to commence on April 18.

The MVD chief was requested to recommend the mode of travel and work out a complete security blue-print.

The story went on to describe a meeting, called by Dmitrov, of strategists, naval experts and security men, including Strelchuk.

It was Strelchuk who suggested that the projected trade mission might provide the opportunity which could tempt the SIS into involving Crabb once more. Dmitrov's interest was caught. Apart from his desire to trap Crabb, whether to liquidate him or pass him over to Strelchuk's Underwater Operations, he wanted to humiliate the British Secret Service.

The SIS had struck the MVD several morale-shattering blows since Beria's demise, and Dmitrov began to see the circumstances of a State visit as the perfect setting for strike at the SIS.

Strelchuk suddenly said: 'Why not the *Ordzhonikidze*? And perhaps it could be accompanied by two of the new destroyers from which our divers could operate to protect it.'

Dmitrov asked: 'What is so attractive about the *Ordzhonikidze*?'

'It is the next of the *Sverdlov*-class cruisers. You remember that Crabb investigated the *Sverdlov*. Perhaps the SIS could be made to think that the *Ordzhonikidze* has more advanced features which are top secret.'

'Such as?'

Strelchuk shrugged. 'I am not a design expert. Perhaps one of these comrades can suggest something?'

Dmitrov looked around the table. 'Comrades?'

Captain Sorokin, head of Naval Intelligence, said: 'Why not some mechanism on the lower hull that would give the ship additional speed or greater manœuvrability? This would tempt any navy in the world.'

Strelchuk nodded enthusiastically.

Dmitrov said to Sorokin: 'Could you have drawings done? And write out a layman's description?'

'Certainly, Comrade General!'

'Excellent! We will feed this information to the press in England as part of the pre-visit publicity.' He turned to Strelchuk. 'And you will have some picked frogmen aboard the destroyers. You will also accompany them to supervise operations.'

'Yes, Comrade General.'

Early in March a British journalist picked up the story of the *Ordzhonikidze*'s secret features from a Russian naval man in West Berlin. It was published, complete with Sorokin's diagrams, by two London dailies.

A few weeks later General Dmitrov received a report from 115. The SIS had grabbed the bait, it said. A recommendation that an underwater inspection be made of the hull of the *Ordzhonikidze* had been put to the SIS by British Naval Intelligence.

Dmitrov prodded the signal with his stubby finger and sat back with something approaching glee. He had dead-drop messages passed to 219 and 115, asking for immediate reports on Crabb.

Rawlins's report came back first. It was not very encouraging. It described the ex-Naval man as a rather sad little man of forty-six, and in poor shape physically. Moreover, he was in impecunious circumstances and almost an alcoholic. It was hard to take him seriously. Rawlins, who was passing himself off as a maritime insurance investigator with plenty of 'expense account' money to spend in bars, was able to stand Crabb to long drinking sessions and even lend him money. He summed up Crabb as a bad security risk, and considered it most unlikely that Crabb would ever be used again by the SIS.

The report from 115 was more encouraging. The operative had been able to gather enough information to state that inside the SIS Crabb was still held in some esteem. Despite his eccentricities and human failings, he was regarded as a discreet and courageous under-water operator highly skilled at his trade.

The head of the MVD read the report with a nod of satisfaction. He regarded it as evidence that the British Secret Service was in a sorry state. With his own man, 115, within its ranks and able to pick off his information targets at will, and with some of its senior officers showing this incredible lack of judgment, the SIS was indeed at a low ebb. Now was the time to strike.

He pressed a buzzer which summoned his personal assistant.

'Slavin. At ten o'clock tomorrow morning I want a meeting with the Head of Operations and Head of Plans. See to it they are here.'

'Yes, Comrade General.'

The next morning in London Chauncey Bowes said:

'It's damnably clever.'

86

'Of course it is. But is it true?'

'I don't know. I don't honestly know.'

'Has C read it?'

'Yes. He's not sure either.'

'Who was 115?'

Bowes shrugged unhappily. 'It could only have been Philby.'

There was a pause.

Evans said: 'What's the next move?'

'Obviously, we've got to see the rest of it.'

'To see their hand will cost ten thousand.'

'Right.'

'So I've got to get the script back to Stringer and tell him it's genuine as far as I can tell. He'll then take it to Brayne-Watts.'

'Yes.'

'Then what?'

'If Brayne-Watts agree to putting up the money, Stringer will have to pay it into the Swiss bank, as directed.'

Evans nodded. Bowes passed him the manuscript and he put it into the brown envelope.

'Yes.'

'Do you want another man?'

'No.'

'You really need one, you know.'

'I don't need anyone.' Evans stood up, anxious to get going.

'What time are you leaving?'

'On the five o'clock plane.'

Bowes stood up. 'Well good luck, Mike.' They looked at each other. 'Want my own opinion?'

'I do.'

'I think it's phoney.'

'That's interesting.'

The two men shook hands.

13

'If you want another whisky you'll have to hurry,' the air-hostess said. 'We'll be at Tempelhof in twenty-five minutes.'

Bentleigh Stringer nodded quickly. 'Then I'll hurry,' he said, beaming up at her.

It was just on evening and he was in a grand mood. While the hostess went off to get another drink he sat back happily and thought: What a fantastic week it's been! It began with Greta, of course, and that quite unforgettable Sunday evening. She'd been in his thoughts ever since. The little moaning sounds she made, her perfume, and her squirming thighs—and the Crabb manuscript.

Bentleigh sipped the whisky and continued to contemplate his good fortune. Evans had turned up yesterday with the Crabb manuscript, reporting that in his opinion it was genuine. He'd agreed to write the foreword. They'd fixed the fee for supervision and editing, plus the foreword, at five per cent of the author's royalty. And Brayne-Watts had agreed to pay the ten thousand pounds advance to Anatoly Marakov. Bentleigh had the bank draft in his wallet now.

The 'Fasten Safety Belts' sign came on. The air hostess wagged her finger at him as she passed up the aisle and he drained the glass and handed it to her as she came back.

The moment he stepped off the plane at Tempelhof he made for the telephones. He dialled Greta's number and felt the thrill of anticipation.

She came on the line, her voice low and cautious.

'Hallo.'

'Bentleigh.'

'Oh!' He grinned as he heard the breathless reaction. 'Hal-lo!' Her voice took on a husky intensity. 'Where *are* you?'

'At the airport.'

'I can't believe it!'

'Would you like to dine out?'

'That would be wonderful!'

'We have something to celebrate.'

'Really?' She sounded incredulous.

'Operation successful, my dear. I have the bacon with me.' He hung up and made his way to Customs.

As soon as he was through he caught a cab to the Hilton, dropped off his case and overnight bag and went on to Schöneberg.

She opened the door and took both his hands and pulled him towards her. He took her in his arms and they kissed passionately. Then with trembling hands she helped him off with his coat.

She had two Martinis ready. As soon as she'd led him to the bar he whipped out his wallet with a flourish and produced the Brayne-Watts draft. It was made out to Anatoly Marakov. She held it up to her eyes, read it, then put it to her lips. Then they raised their glasses and tipped them, meeting each other's eyes across the rims. It was a toast of success, of conquest, shared by conspirators.

She said breathlessly: 'You must tell me everything that's happened! *Everything!*'

Instead, he put down his empty glass, took hers from her and stood it on the bar then picked her up in his arms and carried her upstairs. In the bedroom they stood by the bed and kissed passionately. He was slightly breathless from the exertion. Their hands went down together.

At ten o'clock they went out and dined. Bentleigh chose the luxurious Romansches room in Europa Centre. The lavish twenty-two-storey skyscraper topped by the twirling Mercedes star matched Bentleigh's flamboyant mood. He wanted the biggest and the most expensive. He was dining with the most beautiful girl in Berlin and he wanted the world to see him.

Greta gave him her whole attention. Her large blue-green eyes devoured him. Her hand caressed his. Her legs touched his beneath the table-cloth. Every word she breathed was a message of adoration for all to see. She knew Bentleigh well by now, and exactly how to flatter him and please him.

Over liqueurs, he said: 'Now, darling, what's the next move?'

'Back to bed, I hope.'

He smiled. 'The next move with Anatoly Marakov. When can I get my hands on the rest of the script?'

She became businesslike. 'I will pass the word to my friend that I have seen the Brayne-Watts draft and that it is being paid into a bank in Zürich. When will you pay it in?'

'Tomorrow. In the morning I will fly to Zürich, pay in the draft and open an account in Marakov's name, then fly back. You will dine with me again tomorrow evening?'

She was leaning towards him, her eyes looking into his. 'What do *you* think?'

The following evening when he stepped off the plane in West Berlin Greta was at the airport to meet him. She looked stunning in a deep green tailored suit and a cute off-the-face hat.

The sight of her gave him a twinge of discomfort. To be seen dining with a beautiful girl in a lavish restaurant was different. He was Bentleigh Stringer. It was almost expected of him. But Greta at the airport, coming to meet him, taking his hand in hers, kissing him, and hugging his arm as they walked through the terminal, gave him qualms. It spelled involvement. And there was something else. Her face looked white, her lips stark, her eyes shadowed. She seemed tense, vaguely troubled. An instinct told him that something had gone wrong.

He led her into the terminal cocktail bar. They sat on high stools and had a drink. Champagne.

After an intimate toast, she said: 'I have some ridiculous news, Bentleigh.' A shadow crossed her eyes and her voice shook slightly.

He looked at her keenly. 'Oh?'

'I am *so* upset about it!'

He smiled easily. 'Calm down. Tell me. Is it about the manuscript? If he's fallen down there's still time to have the draft stopped.'

'No, no. Marakov's finished it. He has it ready for you.'

'Well, that's not too ridiculous.'

She hesitated, not quite knowing how to explain it. 'But Marakov's in Krakow.'

'Krakow?'

'In Southern Poland.'

'Well, so what? Can't he send the manuscript to your contact?'

'That's what's so ridiculous. He wants *you* to come to Krakow with the bank receipt and pick up the completed manuscript.'

'I see.'

'He insists that it is quite safe. Plenty of tourists go to Krakow.'

'Yes, but——' Bentleigh broke off and gave a sigh of annoyance. 'What's behind it? What reason does he give?'

'He's been able to move to Southern Poland on account of his health. It's very cold in Moscow at present. So they've let him come as far south as Krakow. But if he tries to cross the border he's sure to arouse the suspicions of the Russian authorities. He wants personally to hand you the manuscript and have you read it while you are there so that he can make any amendments you might want or answer any questions.'

Bentleigh snorted and wriggled on the stool in annoyance. 'That's utter rubbish!'

He drained his glass and ordered another round. He was

shaken. But he managed to keep his feelings to himself, and Greta, watching him carefully, saw no panic. But he felt uncomfortable about it. There was something wrong with it. However, to himself he was saying that he would not be going to Krakow. If Marakov persisted, he'd have the draft stopped, and to hell with his manuscript. He would never put his personal safety on the line for a manuscript, no matter how good it was. But there must be some way round it.

He put a hand on hers and said easily: 'We'll work something out. Don't worry, my love.' He gave her a reassuring smile. Then he asked: 'What are the instructions, exactly?'

'You are to go by train to Krakow. This is quite reasonable. Lots of tourists do this. It's quite a lovely city. You are to stay at the Dom Turysty. Marakov will contact you there.'

Bentleigh wrote down the name of the hotel.

They dined at her apartment that evening. But it wasn't a success. They went to bed, but his heart wasn't in it. The gilt had been scared off the ginger-bread. It seemed to him that her passion had become a nervous intensity, her adoration an over-anxious desire to involve him. He found it faintly cloying and was glad to leave just after midnight and take a cab back to the Hilton.

At eight on Saturday morning, Bentleigh rang Evans at the Europa and asked to see him. When Evans invited him over he breakfasted and arrived at the hotel just after nine. Evans was sipping coffee and sitting by the window smoking. He invited Stringer to have a cup of coffee. Stringer accepted and sat on the other upholstered chair. He told Evans about Marakov's message.

Evans listened in silence. It didn't surprise him. When Stringer had finished he said regretfully: 'That's too bad. It would have made a good book.'

Stringer said: 'You mean I shouldn't go to Krakow?'

'Good heavens, no! Anyway, it's a bloody cheek. Have Brayne-Watts stop the draft and send a message back through your contact that the deal's off.' Evans relit his pipe and blew out the match.

Stringer sipped his coffee in silence for a time. He seemed uncertain how to go on.

Eventually he said: 'Michael. Look. You are now a famous journalist. Your Philby book must have given the KGB a certain amount of satisfaction. Your fame would be your protection. As you've intimated, I *daren't* go. I daren't cross the Wall. Chris West has told me that. I'm the known pipeline used by the underground writers. I *daren't* go! But would *you* consider going?'

Evans was silent for a time. 'I'd like to think about it. Marakov may be playing a dangerous game.'

'What do you mean?'

'I don't know exactly.' After another pause Evans said: 'What's your proposition?'

Bentleigh looked at him without expression. This was what he'd wanted to discuss. A proposition. This was something he could understand. He said: 'An extra thousand sterling for the delivery of the Marakov manuscript.'

Evans was looking out of the window. 'Very well.'

Bentleigh was slightly stunned at Evans's quick reply, but he said casually: 'Do you want it now?'

'Yes.'

Stringer got up and pulled out his cheque-book. He went to the dressing-table and wrote out the cheque. He tore it off, folded it and passed it to Evans. Evans took it and put it in the pocket of his dressing-gown.

He said: 'And I want Marakov's bank receipt.'

'Of course.' Stringer produced it from his wallet and gave it to him. 'What else?'

'The name of the hotel in Krakow.'

'The Dom Turysty. When will you go?'

'Tonight. I think there's a train from East Berlin. And I'm going to need your passport. And your driver's licence.'

Stringer stared at him. 'I don't understand.'

'Marakov doesn't want to see Michael Evans. I'm a published author in the same field. He wouldn't trust me. He will give the manuscript to Bentleigh Stringer.'

'I still don't understand, Michael. How could you possibly pass yourself off as *me*?'

Evans smiled. 'And you an underground literary agent? I shan't *look* like you at all. But I'll look like the picture in your passport.'

Stringer shrugged and waved his arms airily. 'I'll leave it to you. It's quite out of my line.' He produced his passport and driver's licence and gave them to Evans. 'But how do I get on without them?'

Evans stood up. 'I'll tell you all about that later. I'll see you again this afternoon, say, at two-thirty. There are a few things I've got to do before then. I'll see you at the Hilton.'

'Fine. Very much obliged, Michael!'

Bentleigh was still in the Hilton lounge enjoying a liqueur and a cigar after lunch when Evans arrived. They went up to Stringer's suite.

Evans took a passport from his hip pocket and handed it to Stringer.

He said: 'You've got to be Michael Evans for the next forty-eight hours.'

In some trepidation, Bentleigh opened the passport and examined it. His own picture was pasted into it. It looked perfect in every detail, thoroughly authentic.

'I see what you mean. But what do I do? How do I manage it?'

Evans said carefully: 'I want you to get these moves carefully fixed in your brain. I shall leave here shortly. I want you to pack your overnight bag only. Then I want you to ring the switchboard and have them transfer you to the travel department. When you get onto them you ask them if they can book you a seat on the overnight train from East Berlin to Krakow. They either will be able to or they won't. In any case, you get them to ring Krakow and book you the best room you can get at the Dom Turysty.'

Bentleigh nodded.

Evans went on: 'As soon as you've done this, ring the switchboard again and tell them that you are going to Krakow, and that you will be staying at the Dom Turysty, and that anyone who tries to contact you is to be told where you've gone. This is in case your contact rings to check up on you.'

Bentleigh thought ruefully of Greta and nodded. 'I understand.'

'Then I want you to wait until five o'clock. Then you will ring the desk and ask them to order you a cab. When you go downstairs, with only your overnight bag, you will tell the desk that you will be away for two nights and that you've left the rest of your luggage in your room and you want the suite kept booked. Got that?'

'Right.'

'You get in the cab and go to the post office. You pay the cab off, then use a telephone. Look up the classifieds and find yourself a hotel out in Wilmersdorf and book a room in the name of Michael Evans. Then catch a cab and go there. And when you get there, stay in your room. Buy some books and do some reading. Don't make any phone calls. Tell the desk you want a good rest. Have all your meals in your room. Nobody must see you. Understand?'

Stringer nodded bleakly. 'I think so.'

Evans ran through it all again. Then he left the hotel.

Sara Collins burst into Bill Herrara's office.

'You want to see me, chief?'

The U.P. chief stopped typing, pushed his spectacles up on his forehead and looked at her.

'Hi, Sara.'

He put his glasses back on and groped around his large crowded desk and found a pink memo slip.

'One for you, babe. Looks like a good lead. From Ruth Gulliver.'

He gave it to her and looked up at her appreciatively as she sat on his desk to read it. Her green woven body-stocking showed between the tops of her leather knee-boots and her thigh-short tweed skirt. Her short-sighted eagerness always amused him.

She read:

SARA COLLINS/ INTERESTING ANGLE DROPPED BY TALKATIVE PASSENGER ON TRANSATLANTIC FLIGHT/ NAME BENTLEIGH STRINGER/ AUTHORS' AGENT/ CLAIMS HES HOTSHOT CLOAKNDAGGER WHIZZ KID WHO SPENDS HIS TIME PICKING UP MANUSCRIPTS FROM SOVIET UNDERGROUND WRITERS/ STRINGER OPERATES FROM LONDON BUT COMMUTES WEST BERLIN/ GREAT ANGLE IF YOU COULD GET LOOK-SEE AT STRINGER MAKING CONTACT/ POLITICAL CLIMATE JUST RIGHT FOR THIS STORY/ WILL TAKE UP TO 5000 WDS IF STORY STANDS UP/ LOVE KIDDO/ RUTH GULLIVER.

Sara blinked and re-read it. She picked up a pencil from Herrara's desk and sucked it.

'Any good?' Bill asked.

She stood up. 'A ring-dinger, Bill. Thanks!'

She hurried into her tiny office and sat at her desk. Mike Evans was on her mind. Bentleigh Stringer was his agent. She dialled the number of the Europa. When the switchboard answered she asked for Herr Evans.

'Herr Evans has checked out,' she was told.

'Did he say where he was going?'

'No, madam. I presume he has gone back to London.'

Sara hung up. The hound, she thought. Then she thought of Stringer. Evans told her Stringer always stayed at the Hilton. She found the number in her teledex and dialled it with the pencil. The number answered. She asked for Herr Stringer and was told:

'Herr Stringer left the hotel a short time ago.'

Sara gave a desperate sigh for the benefit of the operator. 'Oh, dear! I've missed him!'

The telephonist said: 'I was told to tell anyone who rang that he had gone to Krakow.'

Sara's eyes widened. 'Krakow? You mean in Southern Poland?'

'Yes. He is staying at the Dom Turysty.'

Sara thanked her and hung up.

She poked her head in Herrara's door and said: 'See you, Bill.'

He stopped typing and looked at her. 'Hows about dinner tonight?'

'Not tonight, sweetie. I'll be hot on the scent of Bentleigh Stringer.'

'Attababy. Take it easy.'

He swung back to his typewriter, a man with a deadline.

She closed the door and hurried out of the building, walked down to the Ku-Damm and caught a cab to the Hotel Frühling-am-Zoo.

By the time she'd changed and packed and taken the cab through Checkpoint Charlie, she arrived at the East Berlin Bahnhof only minutes before the train was due to leave. She had to queue up at a counter to buy an East German transit visa, then queue up at another counter for her Polish transit visa. Then she bought a return ticket to Krakow. She had to run to the platform only seconds before the long drab train pulled out.

14

Someone was shaking her gently by the shoulder. She opened her eyes and looked about her, blinking short-sightedly; after the checking of documents at the border she had fallen into an untroubled sleep. She groped for her spectacles and put them on and looked up into a kindly middle-aged face with a straggling yellow moustache.

The guard said something in Polish, something that ended with 'Krakow'.

Sara sat up. 'Krakow? Are we at Krakow?'

He nodded, smiling at her.

She stood up quickly. He reached up and lifted down her case. She thanked him and took it from him and went off quickly down the aisle. The compartment was clear of passengers.

Then she stepped down onto the vast flat station platform. She was almost alone at the end of the long train. The engine had been uncoupled and was standing on a nearby branch-line taking in water.

She began to hurry in some desperate state of urgency. Most of the other passengers had left the station, so she must hurry. Then she stopped, put down her case and looked around her. What was she hurrying for? There was no reason to. She was in Poland. Krakow. This was the locale of her story. She smiled at the thought of Ruth Gulliver's face, if she could see her now. And Bill Herrara. He would have a duck-egg! She must really send him a telegram so that he could mark her position on a map with a pink-headed thumb-tack. She picked up her case and walked up the platform to the wide entrance, where she surrendered her ticket and showed her Polish transit visa.

Outside the station there were no cabs. They must have all been taken by the other passengers. She asked a porter how to get to the Dom Turysty. He said something which included the word 'Westerplatte' and pointed straight ahead along the wide street, then to the right. He said 'Westerplatte' again. She thanked him and began to walk briskly in the freezing air.

The city of Krakow was different from anything she'd seen before. She hadn't seen Russian cities yet and she imagined that some of them must look like this. Under dun clouds, Krakow looked subdued, almost medieval, the architecture Russian in flavour. She stopped and stood still, looking at a great church with a tall spire standing up starkly against the mid-grey sky. She went on through the Market Square. Eventually she found Westerplatte and the Dom Turysty.

She had no difficulty booking a room. The girl behind the desk was Slavic and beautiful, good casting for her story. The tariff was seventy zloty—nearly three dollars a night. As she signed the register she saw the signature of the latest arrival. B. Stringer. Room 134. She booked into 127, also on the first floor.

She went upstairs, unpacked, bathed and changed—fresh underwear, but the same outfit and knee-boots. She put in her contact lenses. Now she put a short-hand notebook into her handbag and stole along the corridor. She found Number 134 and knocked lightly.

The door opened.
It was not Bentleigh Stringer. It was Mike Evans.
She stepped back.
'Evans!'
He stared at her furiously.

99

'What the blazes——' he began softly, but broke off, looking up and down the corridor.

'Mike! I'm looking for——'

He caught her wrist and pulled her savagely into the room and closed the door.

'What the hell are you doing here?'

She stood blinking at him. 'I was following Bentleigh String——'

'You stupid little fool!'

'But, Evans! I didn't know! I didn't *know*! I thought I was following Bentleigh Stringer!'

He stared at her furiously and sucked his teeth in disgust and turned away. He began to unpack his overnight bag.

She stood uncertainly and watched him.

'Evans. I'm sorry. Ruth Gulliver in New York sent me a lead on Stringer and asked me to do a story. When I rang the Hilton they told me he'd gone to Krakow and was booked in at this hotel.'

He put his few clothes into a drawer of the dressing table.

She said: 'Evans. Please don't be angry with me.'

He picked up his towel and shaving gear. He turned and looked at her.

He said: 'Walkley crossed into East Berlin to find out about Stringer. They tore his balls off and shot his guts out!'

He stripped off his shirt and went into the bathroom and shut the door after him.

She sat on the bed.

Then she got up and left the room and closed the door and went along the corridor to her room. She took out her contact lenses, wiped her moist eyes and put on her Betty Boops. She put on her fur coat and hat and strolled out of the hotel.

For the next few hours she went sight-seeing all over the city with the aid of a mimeographed guide-book, printed in English, that she had picked up from the hotel desk. She visited St Florian's Gate and the Barbician, walked through St Mary's Church and knelt before its ornate fifteenth-century

Wit St Woiz Altar, went to the Royal Wavel Castle, the home of Polish kings—and the Jagellonian University, the famous Collegium Maius. Some time later she went into a coffee shop near the Cloth Hall and sat smoking cigarettes and drinking coffee. She had decided to go back to the railway station and inquire about the trains out. Maybe she could get one out through Czechoslovakia. She wasn't annoyed with Evans, she told herself, only hurt that he'd been so rough on her. She thought guiltily of Bill Herrara and decided she'd better send him a telegram or try to ring him to let him know where she was.

'You should never have left the *Des Moines Despatch*,' a voice said. Evans slid into the seat opposite her.

'That's what my father says.'

'I'm glad to hear there's one Collins with some sense. I'll write him a letter.'

'I wish you would. He'd love to hear from you.'

He looked at the checked table-cloth, then raised his eyes to hers. 'Now you know how I got my nose battered. It's my turn to say I'm sorry, Collins.' He looked at the guide-book. 'Have you seen St Florian's Gate?'

'Yes. And the Barbician.'

'So have I.' He said it again: 'Collins, I'm sorry.'

'This city was the capital of Poland once. Did you realize that?'

'Only vaguely, Collins——'

'From the fourteenth to the sixteenth centuries.'

After coffee and toast they strolled back to the hotel.

Outside his door he said: 'Collins. I'm tired. I'm going to lie down for a while.'

'Good. I'll join you.'

They went into his room and took off their coats and lay on the bed. He lay on his back and she rested her head on his arm.

After a long time, she said: 'Evans.'

'Huh?' He was half asleep.

'Tell me something.'

'What?'

'Why are you pretending to be Bentleigh Stringer?'

'Guess.'

'To pick up some underground manuscripts for him. That's right, isn't it?'

'Near enough.'

She raised herself onto her elbow and looked earnestly into his face. 'Why didn't *he* come?'

'Guess again.'

'Because he's frightened?'

He grinned at her and nodded.

She asked: 'Why did *you* come?'

'He paid me a thousand.'

'Is that the only reason?'

'It's enough, isn't it?'

'For Bentleigh Stringer. Not for Michael Evans.'

There was a long pause. He went to sleep. She lay back on his arm.

She said suddenly: 'I don't believe it.' She gave a little wriggle of displeasure and closed her eyes.

After a while he half sat up and looked down into her face. 'Collins.'

She opened her eyes and looked up at him.

'Yes?'

'Lay off this, will you?'

'Lay off what?'

'The story. There's no story in Stringer. He's a womanizing lush. He stumbled onto a good thing through no fault of his own. But writing him up either way will do nobody any good.'

Her large eyes were watching his mouth. She blinked several times.

'Would it harm you, Evans?'

'Yes. It would harm me.'

'Then I won't write it.'

'Thank you. What about a sleep before dinner?'

'You mean what about shutting up?'

'Yes.'

They slept for three hours.

Then they dressed and strolled out into the ice-cold night and found a restaurant. It was built inside an ancient cellar, and was reached by wide stone stairs going down beside one great wall. They ate a very thick dark red beetroot soup, then a kind of *Wiener Schnitzel*, and drank coffee and a coarse red wine. Then they strolled back to the hotel.

When they reached his room he unlocked the door and opened it. An envelope lay on the floor just inside. Evans picked it up. He tore open the envelope and slipped out a note, unfolded it. It was hand-printed in block letters with a ball-point pen. It read:

FOLLOW THE ROAD TOWARD WIELICZKO ON FOOT THREE KILOMETRES OUT OF TOWN. FOLLOW NARROW ROAD OFF RIGHT TWO KILOMETRES TO HOUSE ON LEFT. MEET YOU 10 AM TOMORROW

A M

He grunted, folded the note and put it in his hip pocket. He locked the door and went to his overnight bag. He unzipped it and produced a bottle of Scotch.

'Night-cap?'

She nodded and sat on the bed. After he'd poured the drinks she said: 'That was your contact, wasn't it?'

'Yes.' He sat beside her.

'When does he want to meet you?'

'Tomorrow morning.'

'Is the contact with an underground agent?'

'No. The author.'

'Are authors more reliable than agents?'

'They don't know how to kill expertly.'

'I see.' After a pause she said: 'Evans.'

'What?'

'You're a spy, aren't you?'

'No. I'm a journalist.'

She shook her head slowly. 'No, Evans. You're still a spy.'

He shrugged.

After a time she turned to him and asked: 'Are you married?'

'I was.'

'Divorced?'

He nodded.

'Children?'

He shook his head. They finished their drink slowly, in silence. He got up and poured another. He sat beside her again.

She said: 'Tomorrow. Will it be dangerous?'

'I don't think so.'

Suddenly, he put his drink aside and squatted on his haunches before her and took her hand.

'Collins. Will you do something for me?'

'Yes.'

'I want you to get the first train out of here in the morning. Any train heading West—even via Czechoslovakia. You mustn't hang around Krakow. Do you hear?'

'Yes.' She looked into his anxious questioning eyes and nodded.

He dropped her hand and stood up and got his drink. He walked about the room restlessly. Then he came and sat beside her.

She said: 'Evans. Is what you are doing *worth* anything?'

He thought for a long time. 'If anything in this world is worth anything. I think it's worth something. I don't know.' He sat with his back rounded, his shoulders hunched. 'It's what *they* believe in.'

'Who are *they*?'

'The underground writers. People like Yuli Daniel and Andrey Sinyavsky. Solzhenitsyn. They write what they must because they want to be themselves. But they can't win. They know they can never win. Not physically. Maybe they win spiritually. I don't know.'

'That's why you're here, isn't it? Not the thousand grubby pounds.'

'I'm just the postman—picking up the mail. It's what's *in* the letter that really counts.'

After a silence Sara said: 'And the mail you're picking up tomorrow. Is it worth picking up?'

'I don't know. It may be a cuckoo in the nest. This particular manuscript may be a pack of lies and its author a phoney.' He produced his wallet and slipped out the bank receipt. 'That's the deposit, already paid in.'

She examined it. 'For a speckled egg?'

'Possibly.' He folded the receipt and put it back in his wallet. He returned it to his pocket. 'I can't let a phoney through. It wouldn't be fair to Daniel or Sinyavsky, would it?'

After a time he put their drinks on the dressing-table and took her spectacles off and sat beside her on the bed. He turned and kissed her tenderly. Then they made love and slept together.

15

Snow had fallen during the night and the whole countryside was a white landscape of undulating hills with dark trees etched against the pale grey sky. Evans, a small figure in a gabardine overcoat and a brown hat, his grey slacks tucked into black rubber boots, trudged out of Krakow along the road towards Wieliczko.

Sara had gone to her own room about six o'clock. He'd stopped her at the door and whispered intensely: 'Don't forget what I told you!'

Smiling, she shook her head then kissed him. He watched her hurry down the corridor to her room.

The breakfast tray had arrived at eight-thirty. After he'd eaten he bathed and dressed, putting on his chamois leather shoulder-holster. His Luger was in it now, snug below his left armpit. Also, a Pringle special, a flat knife, was taped to his back, just above the base of the spine.

Walking steadily now, he looked ahead toward the low line of trees. Far away beyond them, he knew, must be a river. He was strangely at peace with himself this morning, as though his purpose in being here was somehow clearer. The outline of the trees looked closer, and everything seemed simpler. He'd never put it into words before, but he knew now that what he'd said about the underground writers was true. And being here on this road this morning was like saying: I'm involved. I declare myself. I'm on your side. You are right in believing that no oppression can be effective without those who are willing to submit to it, and that an even more unpleasant phenomenon than the regime which formed it was the 'creative intelligentsia'—those people who say one thing and mean another. He thought of last night and Sara. It seemed that this morning everything was clear about that too.

He reached the three-kilometre post and went a hundred yards farther on. A narrow road branched off to the right, and he went along it. Before him lay a narrow strip of white that stretched straight and level through a forest of stark leafless trees. He went along it and reached a point where it began to dip. He looked behind him and could see only the summit of the road, a ribbon of white cut through the forest in a swathe.

Presently, he came to a clearing on the left, and standing back a hundred yards stood a house. It was an old farmhouse with walls of timber and whitewashed brick. Behind it was a rising field covered with snow. To the right was a thick forest of dark trees. He turned off the road and went toward the house. A dog barked as he approached. He saw an Alsatian guard-dog chained to a kennel some distance from the road.

He walked up some stone steps onto a wide terrace of flagstones that ran the full length of the house. A black Zil limousine stood in a converted stable, the doors of which were wide open.

He went to the large timber door and knocked.

He heard footsteps inside. They came closer and a bolt shot back and the door opened.

A man stood before him. He was tall, with stooped shoulders, and slightly staring eyes behind horn-rimmed spectacles. He had a lean intelligent face with a high forehead, balding hair and a neatly trimmed dark-brown beard and moustache. He looked like an aesthete, a committed person—committed to an ideology or a love—maybe too committed.

At the sight of Evans he smiled broadly, showing even white teeth, and extended a hand.

He said with surprising softness: 'Bentleigh Stringer! How good of you to come!'

The farmhouse was almost bare of floor coverings. Only the large living-room looked lived-in. It had two black-and-white cow-rugs on the stone floor, and the furniture was sparse and plain. A large log-fire was going in the huge stone fireplace in the end wall. In the wall facing the terrace were three long windows protected on the outside with wrought-iron bars.

Anatoly Marakov had a tray of coffee on a table by the fire. He poured two cups.

'It was good of you to come,' he said again. His English was good, but slightly stilted, with more than a trace of an accent. 'But no doubt it was explained to you.'

'Of course.'

Evans drew out his wallet and produced the bank receipt. He passed it to the Russian, who looked at it for several seconds. It was probably the first real money he'd been allowed to earn from his writings. Evans wondered if he appreciated how much ten thousand pounds sterling really was.

'I cannot believe it,' he said softly. 'I could live for fifteen years on this in Russia!'

He handed Evans his coffee. Then he crossed to the mantelpiece. He took from it a quarto-sized bound manuscript and handed it to Evans.

'My side of the bargain.'

'Thank you.'

Evans opened it and saw the full Crabb manuscript. He made no comment.

Marakov said: 'Now, if I leave you alone you can read it right through.'

Evans nodded. 'That's why I'm here.'

'Good. Then it is no use talking further until you have read it. You agree?'

'Of course.'

As soon as they'd finished their coffee, the Russian stood up.

'I have a chore to attend to. When you feel like some lunch or a drink, just ring this bell.' He indicated the small hand-bell on the mantelpiece. 'Boris will attend to you.' He didn't bother to explain who Boris was.

'Thank you.'

A few minutes later, Evans heard a car start up. He saw the Zil turn from the terrace and follow the narrow track to the road and head toward Krakow.

Evans sat down in front of the fire and began to read *The Making of Korablov*.

16

It was good. Marakov was a facile writer with a flair for marshalling facts and moving the story-line along with ever-mounting interest and suspense. The story stayed with General Dmitrov for a time, following him through the planning conference and the internal political and departmental moves which shaped the operation that was destined to enmesh Crabb and bring about his capture and ultimate defection.

An MVD operative who was given the name of Smith—Matthew Smith—appeared as a seascape artist around the Portsmouth dock area. He was a frequenter of the Keppel's Head, a pleasant inn midway between H.M.S. *Vernon* and H.M. Dockyard. A Russian who'd spent several years in America, Smith—well-spoken, handsome and over six feet tall—posed as an American war-hero. Rawlins brought him into the Keppel's Head one day and introduced him to Crabb. They became a regular threesome. Smith and Crabb had much in common as Smith had been in the U.S. Navy, he claimed. When Smith realized the sorry state of Crabb's finances he began to fund him and give him gifts of bottles of whisky, and the two of them spent a great deal of time together in the evenings.

Meanwhile, 115 had kept Dmitrov in touch with happenings inside the British Secret Service. He reported on April 9 that the SIS officer who had put forward the idea of the underwater inspection of the *Ordzhonikidze* now formally submitted it for clearance to the head of the SIS, 'C', who was about to go on leave. He approved in principle and told the officer to clear the operation with Hugh Matthews, whose job, Evans knew, was to advise the Foreign Office of SIS operations likely to be diplomatically delicate. Evans remembered that on that day Matthews was called urgently away because of family illness—a stroke of luck for the MVD, 115 reported, for Matthews left the office without passing the message on to the Foreign Office official who, Evans knew, would almost certainly have cancelled the operation. Crabb was contacted by an SIS man and offered a fee of fifty pounds. Crabb was disgruntled and wanted more. The SIS man told him he would see what he could do. (This was news to Evans.)

On April 15 General Dmitrov with fifteen MVD men arrived at London Airport aboard a Russian airliner. The General immediately visited the head of Scotland Yard's Special Branch and held a discussion about the security procedures for the coming State Visit. Then, with his retinue, he went to Portsmouth and called on the Chief Constable, who went out of his way to make them welcome and outlined the practical aspects of the arrangements. Dmitrov, apparently satisfied, accepted an invitation to lunch at the Keppel's Head.

That evening there was a crisis. Crabb and Matthew Smith had sundry drinks together, and the frogman bared his soul. He was broke and in debt, and he was disgruntled about the paltry fifty pounds the SIS had offered him. He was considering calling off the deal unless they raised the 'ante'. Smith questioned him closely and found that Crabb had pawned his rubber diving suit for twenty pounds.

The following day Matthew Smith made contact with Dmitrov's party in one of the men's toilets at their hotel. He gave the MVD man a note for his chief warning him that Crabb was likely to call off the deal unless the SIS raised the fee. Dmitrov held a meeting with him in his bedroom and instructed him to reveal himself to Crabb in the role of a CIA man and pay him two hundred pounds to examine the hull of the *Smotryashchi*. He gave Smith a clipping from an obscure Swiss magazine which referred to the Russian destroyer being fitted with an asdic dome on each side of the lower hull.

The following evening Smith met Crabb at the Keppel's Head and revealed his 'true' identity. He told Crabb that the CIA was vitally interested in examining the lower hull of the *Smotryashchi* and showed him the magazine clipping. Crabb readily agreed to undertake the job and Smith paid him one hundred pounds in advance.

On April 17 Crabb and his SIS contact called on the Chief Constable, identified themselves and announced the reason for their presence in Portsmouth. The Chief Constable, worried, checked with MI5 and was asked to give them all necessary help; this included provision of an office and Dockyard passes. (Evans could imagine the discomfiture of the Chief Constable and, equally, how impossible it would be for him to refuse police co-operation.)

Commander Crabb and the SIS man, warned that the Russian security party were patronizing the Keppel's Head, booked in at the nearby Sallyport Hotel. Then they spent the rest of the day testing the naval diving apparatus Crabb was to use; this was of oxygen re-breathing type which had the advantage of not producing a revealing trail of air-bubbles but could not be used safely at a depth greater than 33 feet.

That day was the eve of the arrival of the three ships. Sir Anthony Eden checked and rechecked the final arrangements for the State Visit. He had taken the precaution of issuing an instruction that SIS must leave the Russian visitors alone, indicating that the visit was too important politically to be put at risk.

Dmitrov, anticipating such a move, contacted 115 by dead-drop and instructed him to watch for a memorandum from Downing Street. The operative hovered around Hugh Matthews's office and saw the message arrive. Casually, he re-routed it into the wrong channel. It never did reach the adviser's desk.

Evans nodded bleakly as he read it. This was the weakness

of intelligence organizations—the principle of internal secrecy. He could easily understand that if the man responsible for the operations did not receive the Prime Minister's memorandum there would be no other officer in the know about the operation who could take action to stop it.

April 18 dawned. The *Ordzhonikidze* docked at Portsmouth, with her two attendant destroyers, *Sovershenny* and *Smotryashchi*, alongside. Marshal Bulganin and Comrade Krushchev travelled by special train to London. They were met at Victoria Station by Sir Anthony Eden and high government officials. Claridge's Hotel became their London headquarters.

'You want your lunch now, Comrade?' a voice said in Russian. Evans turned to see a big man standing in the doorway. He was dressed in a coarse black shirt done up at the neck and black trousers.

'Are you Boris?' Evans asked in Russian.

The man nodded. He was thick-necked, with the sloping shoulders of a wrestler.

Evans rose and stretched. 'Thank you, Boris.'

He put the manuscript aside and stood by the fireplace. Boris withdrew and reappeared shortly with a bottle of Vodka on a tray with a glass and a wooden plate with chunks of cheese on it.

Evans poured himself a drink and ate some of the cheese while he watched the Russian set the table and bring in the lunch. It was half a chicken on a plate with steaming hot roast potatoes, and fresh brown bread with creamy butter. Boris withdrew without a word and closed the door.

Evans sat down and ate the meal leisurely. He thought about the manuscript. He had to admit that it rang true, but he still had reservations. He found himself anxious to get to the actual dive. For fourteen years the world had conjectured about what really happened on a secret operation that had failed, supposedly killing the operator. He thought: Am I about to learn the truth at last?

After a time Boris brought in a pot of coffee and put it on the table. He stoked the fire and put another log on it and took away the dishes and went out and closed the door. Evans poured himself a cup of coffee and lit his pipe. He sat by the fire and went on reading.

Before dawn on April 19 Commander Crabb and his SIS contact entered the Dockyard. Crabb put on his diving gear, and entered the water of a small boat harbour out of sight of the Russian vessels.

He went under water about eighty yards and stopped, hovering, and made out the dark shape of the *Ordzhonikidze* not far away. He went forward a few yards and swept along just below the curve of the hull. Then he went deeper. He neared the stern, expecting to find the protrusions that had been illustrated in the newspaper article. There was nothing. He gave a snort of disgust and went completely under the cruiser. There was nothing that was different from the hull of the *Sverdlov*. The Ruskis were having them on, and the SIS had fallen for it. Now the *Smotryashchi*——

Suddenly he was choking and there was a rush of sound in his ears. He struggled upwards. His breathing gradually came back to normal. He turned round and retraced his course.

He reached the landing-stage of the boat harbour and struggled up the steps and sat down and tugged off his head-gear and gulped is neveral lungfuls of the cold fresh air.

The SIS man came to his side.

'Okay?' he asked anxiously.

It was a few seconds before Crabb could speak.

'Trouble,' he mumbled. 'Trouble with my—breathing gear.'

He waited two or three minutes regaining his composure and clearing the excess carbon-dioxide from the re-breather. Then he readjusted his headgear and slipped into the water. This time he went out about thirty yards away from the dock-side. He sent himself along until he could see the dim shape of the *Smotryashchi*'s hull. He went down in a long smooth dive.

There was no sign of an asdic dome. He went up and down on each side. The Russians had led the CIA up the garden path too. He thought wryly of Matthew Smith and grinned. He came to the stern of the destroyer. Task completed.

Suddenly a light flashed in a pale beam towards him. A black wriggling figure came at him. Arms came around his neck from behind and pulled him backwards. He kicked at the figure hovering above him. More hands grabbed his legs and something hard caught him across the side of the head. He went backwards and down and down into blackness. He fought for breath and there was a roar in his ears . . .

Crabb opened his eyes.

He was looking into a passive face. The man wore white overalls.

'How do you feel, Comrade?'

Crabb swallowed and looked beyond the man. He was in a ship's cabin. There was something different about it. It was white, and it smelt like a hospital.

'Where am I?'

'Aboard the *Smotryashchi*.'

Crabb listened and heard the throb of engines.

The man said: 'We are taking you back to Russia.'

Crabb stared at him helplessly. 'Oh, Christ!' he muttered and closed his eyes.

Evans read on. On the way back to Russia, Crabb was interrogated by Colonel Mayassov, one of Dmitrov's men. Crabb was given the choice of death or service in the Red Navy. Shocked and in a poor state physically, he asked for time to think about it. When the ships arrived back in Russian waters, he was flown to Moscow and put in solitary confinement in Lefortowo prison. His identification number was 147.

Mayassov came to see him again and asked for his decision. Crabb said he would agree to joining the Red Navy on condition that he would never be asked to spy on the ships of his own country. A week later he was told that the condition had been accepted. Commander Strelchuk came to see him and told him that he was being assigned as an instructor to the Underwater Operational Command at Sevastopol. His new name would be Lvev Lvovich Korablov.

The MVD was faced with the problem of finding a body as a substitute that could be planted where it would be found by the British authorities. They instituted a search throughout Soviet prison camps and found a man of Crabb's approximate age, skin texture and blood-group, and of similar physical characteristics. The unfortunate man was Kuprik Mikulitsin, who had been arrested on suspicion of subversive activities in 1953.

Marakov gave the gruesome details of how Mikulitsin was drowned. How they put Crabb's diving clothes on the corpse. How the corpse was taken to Leningrad and placed in a tank full of salt water, where it had remained for a year. As an obvious precaution against identification, they cut off the head and hands. Then the body was taken by submarine to a carefully calculated point in the English Channel and released. The date was May 25, 1957.

On June 9 a body was found drifting near Pilsey Island in Chichester Harbour, about fifteen miles from Portsmouth. It was badly decomposed, middle-aged. It wore Crabb's diving clothes.

The coroner's finding was that the body was that of Commander Crabb. It was not possible to find as to the cause of death . . .

Today, Crabb is still with Strelchuk and has attained the rank of Captain in the Special Task Underwater Operational Command at Scvastopol, where his dash and courage have established him as an eminent and admired officer. He has even become a minor folk hero about whom a song is sung called 'Korablov the Frogman'. In any convivial night in the naval mess at Sevastopol you are likely to hear:

> Once there lived a seaman free
> A hero who went under the sea!

Legend says he's still under the sea
But here he is right here with me:
Korablov the frogman.

Mike Evans put the manuscript aside and stood up. His pipe had gone out and he knocked it on the hearth and emptied the charred tobacco into the fire. So far so good, he thought. Short of producing Crabb and putting him on show, Marakov could do little more to prove that the English frogman was alive. His narrative had presented much of what was known to be true and seemed at first reading completely believable. It cleared up a number of mysteries including why Crabb was seen under the *Smotryashchi*.

But now he ceased thinking about Crabb and the manuscript. He thought of Anatoly Marakov. What did he want of Evans? Or, rather, of Bentleigh Stringer? Was it something more than just the money? Evans looked out of the window toward the road and decided he needed some fresh air and a stroll after his five or six hours of concentration. He put his pipe in his pocket and strolled to the door. He took hold of the black iron door-knob and turned it.

It was locked.

He tried it again and rattled the knob. It wouldn't budge.

Now he closed his fist and knocked heavily on the thick wooden slats. There was no sound, no answering footstep.

He knocked again.

After a long pause, he drew the Luger from his shoulder-holster, pointed it at the lock and fired. Then he kicked the door open.

He stepped into the corridor, the acrid smell of gunpowder in his nostrils.

He saw Boris, but too late. The Russian brought down the butt of his rifle heavily across Evans's skull. Evans fell sideways into the blackness.

17

Evans woke up. He was lying in blackness on a cold grimy floor of stone, and around him was the dankness of a cellar. His head was throbbing in violent waves of pain. After a time, he felt for his Luger. It was gone. He sat up and put a hand to the base of his spine. His knife was still there, taped in its plastic scabbard to the skin of his back.

He felt through his pockets and found a box of matches. He slid it open and got a match out, closed the box and struck the match. He stood up and found that he was in a large cellar completely bare of furniture. There was straw scattered around the filthy stone floor. Its walls were a grimy grey. They had once been whitewashed. The ceiling consisted of heavy floor-boards above huge rough-hewn rafters. A single electric light bulb hung from the centre, far out of reach. The match went out and he struck another. He saw the stone steps that led up to a heavy timber door. There was no sign of a light-switch. As he stood on the steps the match went out. He sat down and waited, listening.

After a long time he heard a dog barking in the distance. Then he heard the sound of a motor, and tyres on the flag-stones of the terrace.

Presently there were some footsteps, then voices.

Suddenly a bolt was shot back and the door above him opened. A shaft of light was thrown down the steps. He rose quickly and saw a man silhouetted in the light. He came down the steps. It was Marakov.

'My deepest apologies, comrade!' he said. 'Boris did not understand!'

Evans looked at him stonily.

Marakov took his arm to help him up the steps. 'This place is sometimes used as a temporary detention centre, and Boris is the permanent guard. He did not understand that you were my guest! Do please accept my humblest apology!'

They had reached the top of the steps and stood in the small square hall. Boris was standing with his back to the wide front door, his automatic rifle held across his chest. He watched Evans mutely.

Evans said: 'I want my Luger.' He repeated it in Russian.

Marakov told Boris to give the gun back to Evans. Boris took the automatic from his pocket sullenly and handed to Evans.

Marakov was nervous as he ushered Evans into the living-room.

There was a thickset man standing with his back to the fireplace. He had a square-jawed face with a long upper lip and cold hard eyes. He was dressed in a plain grey uniform buttoned up to the neck.

As they approached the fireplace Marakov said: 'Comrade Kovarsky. This is Mister Bentleigh——'

The man said softly: 'Michael Evans. The man who sold out the SIS.' He smiled, and the two men regarded each other. The name had registered with Evans. Kovarsky, Department S, General Zadikov's Chief of Operations. Alex Kovarsky, former secretary of the Russian Writers' Union, later working for Smersh seeking out and arresting underground writers. Chauncey Bowes had described him as the most dangerous man in Department S. 'The man you'll have to watch out for.'

Anatoly Marakov was staring at Evans. 'You are not Stringer?' He turned helplessly to Kovarsky. 'I don't understand, Comrade!'

Kovarsky chuckled, ignoring Marakov. 'Your erstwhile

colleague, Timothy Hannifin, assured me you would be here in Stringer's place. He must know you very well.'

Evans said shortly: 'He should.' He sat on the divan in front of the fire. He looked up at Marakov. 'I've read your Crabb saga.'

'Ah, yes,' Kovarsky said softly.

Marakov asked nervously: 'What did you think of it?'

'Quite remarkable.'

The author looked vastly relieved and turned to look at Kovarsky's reaction.

Kovarsky turned to him patronizingly. 'There, Anatoly! You have done your work well.' He said to Evans: 'And you think it will be published in the West?'

'I am certain. It is quite a remarkable document. One thing is missing, of course.'

'What is that?'

'Proof that Crabb is still alive. You'll have to produce Crabb in Moscow before half a dozen international journalists.'

The two Russians exchanged a smile.

Kovarsky said: 'We intend to do more than that, comrade.' He smiled craftily at Marakov, and nodded.

Marakov turned and crossed to a small table. A 16-millimetre movie-projector was set up on it. The Russian pressed a switch and a beam of light threw a white rectangle onto a screen that hung from a tripod stand at the far end of the room. Marakov focused and brought up the rectangular shape clear and sharp. Then he crossed and switched off the room lights.

Kovarsky arranged two chairs side by side and invited Evans to be seated.

Marakov came back to the projector, checked the threading of the film nervously and turned to look at Kovarsky, who nodded and took a seat beside Evans.

Marakov flicked over a switch and the machine began to operate with a whirring sound. A series of black-and-white hieroglyphs came up on the screen, followed by a count-down of numbers from nine to one, then, as sea-shanty music swelled in, a white-on-black film title:

BRITISH FROGMAN SERVES
IN RUSSIAN NAVY

The opening shot showed the Thames in heavy weather. It was poor quality film, Evans thought, a copy from a 35-mm. print without the use of the negative. A typical British news-commentator said:

'In a bid to save the British seamen trapped in the Royal Navy submarine, *Truculent*, lying helplessly at the bottom of the Thames, Commander Lionel Crabb, British war-hero, dived through the fierce tide.'

There was more commentary while the camera gave shots from various angles showing the early morning activity on the Thames around the spot where the submarine had sunk. Police and Naval craft moved into the area. A frogman came up out of the lashing water. Now he was seen somewhere on shore, his headgear off. He was sitting in a room drinking coffee. A newsreel interviewer asked him several questions. Crabb gave terse monosyllabic answers.

The scene changed, and the music became sweeping and adventurous, like the sound-track of a Hollywood sea-saga. A diver surfaced beside a trawler in a choppy ocean. He was hoisted aboard. The commentator said:

'Diving for Spanish gold off the Isle of Mull, off the Scottish coast, Commander Lionel Crabb kills two birds with one stone by also testing new diving equipment for the British Navy.'

A closer shot showed Crabb smoking a cigarette. He gave short matter-of-fact answers to an interviewer's questions. His voice was terse, with a slight nasal quality.

Another change of scene, and the music is Russian. An atomic submarine surfaces. Now a medium shot shows the conning tower. A man steps out. He wears a black rubber dry-suit. As the camera tracks to him it is seen that it is Commander Lionel Crabb. Evans strained forward to watch, and Marakov stole a glance at his tense profile.

The man held a pack of cigarettes. He took one out, made to put it in his mouth. Instead he gave a grin and threw the cigarette and the pack into the sea. He looked at the camera and said:

'I nearly forgot. I've given up that lot.' Evans strained to listen. It was Crabb's voice, or a damned good imitation. 'I don't smoke any more. And I don't drink too much either. I found it made me short of breath under water. Though, mind you, I don't dive much these days. I leave it to the young 'uns.'

He turned and gave a signal. A line of frogmen came jogging out of the conning tower. They passed Crabb and jumped into the water one by one. The camera panned to a close-up of Crabb. He said:

'Sorry about all the hullaballoo I caused back home. I didn't plan it that way. My friend Matt Smith did. Matt, I spent a few weeks lying on my back in the destroyer's sick-bay hating your guts!' He grinned. 'But, Matt, thanks. You did me a good turn. I was finished back in Britain anyway. I wanted to remain in the Navy, but after the war they retired me. Wasn't gentleman enough for the peace-time Navy. They only wanted my guts in the war. Anyway, I'm glad to be here in Russia. I'm in the pink of condition and I'm happy. Thanks, Matt, old pal.'

The camera moved back and upwards, no doubt from a helicopter. Crabb was seen, a small black figure standing alone on the sub, as male voices swelled in. They were singing 'Korablov the Frogman'.

The film cut out. Marakov switched off the machine and crossed to the wall and switched on the room lights. He turned toward Evans, his face tensed with triumph.

Evans stood up and groped for his pipe.

Kovarsky stood up with him. He was watching Evans closely.

Evans said: 'All right. I'm convinced. I will need to take a copy of that film back to London with me.'

Marakov turned to Kovarsky. 'He can take *this* copy, Comrade.'

Kovarsky nodded. 'He *could*, if that were in the plan. However'—he walked a few paces and stood with his back to the fireplace—'we have other plans for Mr Evans.'

Marakov said: 'I don't understand, comrade.'

Kovarsky said softly: 'Comrade Marakov. You have done your work well. I am very pleased. You are not concerned with the higher planning. Sit down and keep your mouth shut.'

The author stood uncertainly. He stole a look at Evans. Then he sat down and looked into the fire.

Kovarsky turned to Evans. 'Comrade. We are not concerned with getting this manuscript to the West. We can do this a dozen ways. And there is always Mr Stringer and his charming contact in West Berlin. That presents no problem to us. The most important element in this discussion is not Marakov's manuscript. We may even decide that it shall never see the light of day. Or we can decide to produce it at a time when it will embarrass the British Government—perhaps when the United States needs positive guarantees about the efficiency of their ally's security services.'

Marakov had turned slowly to look up at him. His staring eyes had a glazed look in them.

Kovarsky went on: 'No. The *only* important element in this operation is Mr Evans himself. This is the way it was planned. Your friend Timothy Hannifin has convinced us of your value, Mr Evans. We want you in Moscow. Let us put it this way, Comrade. You have been recruited.'

Evans nodded. 'To Department S.'

'Ah. You know about S, do you? We were wondering about that, particularly with your new role as a journalist who has embarrassed the SIS. This makes you very valuable to us as an émigré author working in Russia. Quite a switch, don't you think?'

Evans shrugged.

Kovarsky said: 'For instance, this Crabb manuscript. How much more convincing would it be if it were written by Michael Evans. First his Philby exposé, now Commander Crabb——'

Marakov had risen, his face working with uncontrolled rage. 'You cannot do this, Comrade! I will not permit it!'

Kovarsky said serenely: 'Comrade. Your talents and your toil belong to the Motherland. What happens to them ultimately is for the good of the State. There is no room in our society for the cult of personality. Sit down and do not say another word. That is an order!'

Marakov swallowed. He stood looking at the floor then slowly sat down.

Kovarsky said: 'And you, Mr Evans, will be returning to Moscow with us in the morning.'

Evans said: 'What possible use can *I* be to you?'

'You can help us tell the truth to the world.'

'What do you call the truth?'

'History. The ultimate truth. The inevitable course of history.' When Evans looked heavenwards, the Russian said: 'I am not speaking of obvious propaganda. That's no longer necessary. We have teachers in universities already teaching an inevitable philosophy for the world.'

'You mean absolute control by one mind?'

'Yes. The *people*'s mind.'

'There's no such thing. It's totalitarianism either way. It doesn't matter whether it's national-socialism or Bolshevism. The result's the same.'

Kovarsky snorted. 'So you prefer anarchy by splinter groups? That's the only future for Democracy!'

'It's better than an ant-State that devours human beings as though they're a low-grade substance.'

'You are speaking now of the inferior individuals and groups who resist the order of things!'

Evans nodded. 'This is how you regard your writers, isn't it? As idiots, deceivers and criminals?'

'We *have* to deal harshly with them because of their ill-will, inferior origin, wrong class-consciousness and false convictions! We put them away because we do not need them. We will take the world of tomorrow without them because of the unalterable truth of history——'

'Like a murderer takes a corpse.'

Kovarsky was about to continue the argument. Instead, he swung about and picked up the bell from the mantelpiece. Immediately, the door opened. Boris stepped in, his submachine-gun held easily across his body.

Kovarsky said in Russian: 'Lock him up!'

Evans turned slowly. He looked at Kovarsky and measured the distance to Boris.

Kovarsky said softly: 'The bullets have been removed from your gun, if this information is of any interest.'

Evans crossed the room and walked past Boris, who held his gun on him every step. He went into the hall and turned right. The door to the cellar stood open. He went down the steps into blackness. The door banged behind him and the bolt shot across. He sat down on the bottom step.

A long time later he heard a dog barking.

Then there were odd sounds of footsteps and voices, then a long silence.

There were sudden footsteps in the hall, and the light in the cellar came on.

Evans stood up as the door opened.

Boris's huge figure loomed above, starkly silhouetted in the bright light of the hall. He was dragging someone after him. With a sudden movement he thrust his arm forward and sent Sara Collins down the steps into Evans's arms. The door slammed and the light went off.

18

Evans took both her arms savagely.

He said: 'You didn't get on that train!'

She said hysterically: 'Oh, Mike! Don't yell at me! Please!'
She put her arms round his waist and hugged him.

'Oh, Evans,' she whispered. 'What's going to happen to us?'

He put his arms round her and held her gently. After a time he groped for his matches and lit one. He sat her down on the bottom step. Then when the match went out he squatted beside her and she leaned against his shoulder.

Presently she said in a little voice: 'I was booked on the four-ten train for East Berlin. I came out of my room and walked along the corridor and saw your door open. I heard Russian voices, so I ran back to my room and hid behind the door and watched. I saw two Russians come out. I saw them leave and followed them downstairs. They got into a black car and drove off.

'My taxi was waiting to take me to the station. I got the driver to drive in the direction I'd seen the black car go. It went out of Krakow along a straight flat road. I could see the black car ahead. About three kilometres out, it turned at a road that branched off to the right.

'I got the driver to turn round and take me back to the station where I cloaked my case. Then I walked back along the road. It was getting dark as I arrived at the spot where I saw the car turn off. I walked along about another two kilometres, and on the left I saw a light. I stopped and waited until it was dark.'

Evans asked: 'And what were you going to do?'

'I don't know.' She hugged him. 'Anyway, I don't care. I wouldn't want to live without you, Evans.'

'You'll probably get your wish. What did you do then?'

'I crept toward the house. Suddenly a guard-dog barked and a big man came out and caught me.'

After a time, Evans rose in the blackness. He put a hand behind his back and pulled up his shirt. He gripped the handle of the knife and drew it out of its plastic scabbard.

He said: 'What's happening upstairs?'

Sara said: 'The tall man with the beard was out at the car. And the horrible thickset man with eyes like a fish had his overcoat on. They looked as though they were leaving.'

He sat down beside her and they waited for a time.

Presently they heard the sound of a motor. Then there was the sound of tyres passing over flagstones. The throb of the motor died away.

After a time, Evans put the knife against the wall on the third step. He got up and lit a match. He began to kick the straw across the floor into a central heap. He got Sara to stand aside while he gathered it up and took it up to the top of the stairs. He piled it on the landing against the door.

Sara asked: 'What are you going to do?'

Evans came down to her in the darkness.

He said: 'With Kovarsky and Marakov away the odds are shorter. I've got a chance against Boris. I've got to take it.'

He moved across the cellar in the blackness and lit a match. He stood directly beneath the light bulb.

He said: 'Come here.'

She moved towards him as the match went out. He felt her hands grip his arms.

'I want you to remove the light bulb from its socket.'

He squatted on one knee and put her on his shoulder. Then he rose and lifted her above his head in the pitch blackness.

'Can you reach it?'

Her voice came through the darkness. 'Just a minute. I can't find it. Yes, I've got it!' There was a pause. 'Okay.'

He lowered her to the floor. Then he took her to the wall the door was in.

He said: 'The moment Boris steps into view on the landing I want you to throw the bulb as hard as you can at the opposite wall.' He held her hand and swung it gently in the direction he meant. 'And don't be frightened,' he said lightly. 'The odds are in our favour.'

'You could have fooled me.'

'Two to one.'

He went back to the steps, felt his way up them, groped on the third step and found the knife. He went up to the landing and listened for a minute or so. There was no sound.

He lit a match and looked about him. He caught the two tiny glints from Sara's spectacles below him in the darkness. Running along the wall from the top step was a heavy iron pipe, a relic of some past heating system. He put his foot on it and tried it with his weight. It was solid. He turned now and stood with one foot on the landing and the other on the pipe, his back solidly against the wall. In this position he could hold the knife in his right hand and get leverage from the wall.

He slipped the knife under his left arm and held it flat against his body while he lit a match. He stooped and put the flame to the base of the pile of straw. Then he straightened and gripped the handle of the knife in his right hand.

The flame caught the straw with a crackling sound. He waited until it was a solid blaze and the smoke was escaping under the door into the hall. Then he banged the door sharply with the steel handle of the knife.

The smoke had begun to fill the cellar and an acrid smell assailed his nostrils. The fire was rapidly burning itself out, and as the straw collapsed into black powdery ash he scraped the last of the straw closer to the door.

Footsteps came quickly into the hall.

The light switch clicked.

The heavy iron bolt shot back with a bang.

Evans, flattened against the wall, gripped the knife tensely, holding it low.

The door swung open and light flooded in. The huge shadow of a man was thrown onto the stone steps.

It was Boris. He uttered an exclamation at the sight of the black cellar. He kicked the last of the straw away and stepped in, his gun held tensely forward, his eyes narrowed as he tried to size up the situation. He came level with Evans now. Evans held his breath. He could hear the Russian breathing. There was a pause as he licked his lips. The smoke was hurting his eyes and he blinked.

Pop! The light bulb hit the opposite wall with the sharp flat explosion of a fire-cracker, followed by a tinkle of splintered glass.

In a quick reflex action Boris swung the gun and fired in the direction of the sound.

Evans lunged. The knife flashed in the darkness. The blade entered the Russian's body just below the ribs and pushed up toward the heart. It went up to the hilt and blood gushed over Evans's hand. He pulled it out dripping red.

The big man gave a convulsive sob and sagged to his knees and fell down the steps, the gun clattering to the stone floor. Evans heard Sara give a strangled cry of horror. He threw the knife into the hall and stepped past Boris and went down and picked up the sub-machine-gun. He stood in the light and held out his one clean hand and Sara ran to him, her face averted from Boris's sprawling body. Blood was gushing from the wound and running down the steps and spreading onto the floor. He swung Sara over his shoulder and carried her up the steps and took her into the living-room. He sat her down on the divan in front of the fire then poured her half a glass of Vodka.

He thrust the drink in front of her face. 'Drink this!'

She looked up at him, blinking. Then she looked at the glass and took hold of it with both hands. They were trembling. She brought the glass to her lips.

Gun in hand he went back into the hall and picked up the knife. He took it into the primitive-looking kitchen and washed it under the tap. Then he washed his hands and dried them and the knife. He put the knife back in its scabbard and tucked his shirt into his trousers.

He went back to the living-room and picked up the manuscript and the spool of film. Then he found Sara's handbag on the floor beside the divan. He poured himself half a glass of Vodka and drank it. Then he put the glass down and took Sara's from her and put it on the mantelpiece. He put the spool of film in her handbag and handed it to her with the manuscript. Then, gun in hand, he took her by the arm and went into the hall and out of the front door, leaving the lights on. They went out onto the terrace and turned right toward the opposite end to the garage. He went around the corner of the building and stood in the darkness beside the wall. Sara stood close to him and he put his arm around her shoulders.

About half an hour later they heard the distant sound of a motor. It gradually grew louder, and presently the beam of a car's headlights lit the road. The Zil came into view, slowing down. It turned off at the clearing and came slowly along the drive, turned in onto the terrace and stopped.

The motor cut out and the back door swung open and Kovarsky got out. He stood looking about him with his hands in the pockets of his overcoat. Then a front door opened and Marakov slid from the driver's seat. The other back door opened and a third man climbed out. He was fair-haired and he wore an expensive grey overcoat with wide lapels. Evans heard Sara give a gasp of dismay. It was Tim Hannifin.

19

Gun in hand, the barrel pointing dead at Kovarsky's heart, Evans stepped out into the light of the terrace.

'Hold it there!'

The three men froze in their tracks. Kovarsky uttered a startled exclamation.

Marakov screamed: 'Don't shoot! Don't kill me! I came here to defect!'

Kovarsky whirled on him. 'You scum!'

His hand jerked from his pocket, holding an automatic.

There were two shots, almost simultaneous. Marakov clutched his side and crumpled up onto the flagstones. And Kovarsky stiffened, shot in the back. He fell backwards onto the bonnet of the car and rolled off onto the ground, dead. His smoking gun slid across the flagstones.

Hannifin, his Beretta smoking, held up his hand to Evans. He threw the automatic onto the ground in front of him.

Evans stood like a statue, the tommy-gun trained on Hannifin.

Hannifin put a finger to his lips and crossed quickly to Marakov's body. He knelt beside it and examined it. After a few seconds he looked over at Evans.

'Wounded in the side. Still breathing. But he's unconscious. Maybe hit his head when he fell.' He rose and stood looking at Evans. 'Hullo, Mike.'

Evans stood still, covering him. Sara came out of the shadows and went to his side. At the sight of her Hannifin uttered a gasp.

'Sara!' He ignored Evans's gun and came to them. He snapped at Evans: 'What the blazes is *she* doing here?'

Evans said softly: 'Ask her.'

Hannifin said: 'You must be out of your mind, bringing her here!'

Evans stood looking at him, at his Russian clothes, at his tense white face and anxious eyes.

He said: 'I don't read you, Hannifin.'

Hannifin looked at Sara, trying to read some meaning into her staring eyes. He saw only shock as she blinked at him, her lips slightly parted. She stood and hung onto Evans's arm and not saying anything. He turned to Evans.

'Mike. I'm sorry. I hated myself for leaving you like that in Vienna. The knife job was nothing to do with me. That was Eisendrath. He was smarter than I gave him credit for.'

Evans remained silent.

Hannifin said: 'Look. You sent me in against Eisendrath, didn't you?'

Evans looked at him. 'Yes.'

'But you thought it was an ordinary espionage or counter-espionage operation. Well, it wasn't. Doctor Eisendrath is no ordinary brainwashed Marxist. His stake is higher. He didn't want me as one of his spy-ring. He wanted my brain. My intellect. I realized this at our third or fourth meeting. He began to show me that the so-called free societies would destroy themselves by their very freedom of choice—by anarchy, assisted by a so-called free press——'

Mike said impatiently: 'This is rubbish, Tim.'

Hannifin went on: 'From a document I stole from his desk I learned that his instructions came from one source—Department S.'

Evans stared at him. '*You* knew about S?'

Hannifin nodded. 'From the document. So I decided to join it. That's why I defected.' He put a hand in his pocket and produced a tiny metal cylinder. 'Mike. This is a microfilm. It contains the complete charter and *modus operandi* and immediate targets of Department S. I want you to give it to C.'

'To C?' Evans said bitterly. 'To C?'

'Yes.'

'C knew all about your pretended defection, didn't he?'

'Yes. I didn't tell you, but I shot across to England one day and saw him. He approved and checked it out with me.'

'And with Chauncey Bowes? They put you over to him?'

'Yes, Mike. I'm sorry. But it wouldn't work any other way. You had to play it straight.'

Evans looked at him for several seconds. He said quietly: 'Sure I did. I was the old-fashioned spy with only my outmoded integrity to hang on to. So MI5 had me go through all the copy-book procedure, while you, the new breed, conducted the fight on the level of the intellect. That's right, isn't it?'

Hannifin met his look and nodded. He turned to Sara. 'Sara, I meant what I said about wanting you to join me in Moscow.'

She hid her face in Evans's shoulder. 'I don't want to talk about it,' she mumbled.

Evans said: 'What about that letter?'

Hannifin said: 'It was written for Kovarsky. He thought it was terrific. Sara's article was wonderful. But Kovarsky didn't like it.' He grinned.

'You bastard,' Evans said softly. He looked about the terrace, at the two still figures. Marakov was still unconscious. He said: 'All right, Tim. What's our chances of getting out of here? Spell it out.'

Hannifin said: 'There's an Opel hidden in the trees one kilometre the other side of Krakow on the road to Katowice. You'll find it fifty yards this side of the kilometre post. You can take the Zil and abandon it there and go on in the Opel. It's got enough gas to get you to Berlin. But don't try to get through Checkpoint Charlie in it. They might have traced it by the time you get there.'

'How did you come by it?'

'I bought it in Wieliczka. I came on an earlier plane than I was scheduled on and caught a taxi to Wieliczka. I bought the Opel second-hand, drove it through Krakow and hid it, then walked back to the Krakow Airport. I was waiting there when Kovarsky and Marakov arrived to pick me up.' He put a hand in his pocket and produced a car key. 'Here. Take the key.'

Evans pocketed it, watching him carefully. 'What's it all about?'

'Kovarsky came here to get *you*. He wanted me to be here for the kill, because I planned the whole operation. So I came here to give you the microfilm and help you get away.'

'What about Marakov?'

'You can take him with you if you like, if he really wants to defect. He could be handy to Chauncey, and it would be a further victory over Department S.'

Evans looked down at the unconscious writer, who was making a low moaning sound and stirring slightly. 'What about *you*?'

Hannifin said: 'I'll be all right. I'm after Kovarsky's job. Is that aiming too high?'

'Well, I recruited you.'

They looked at each other and grinned. Then Hannifin said: 'You'll have to shoot me too, Mike. But don't kill me, will you?'

'I'll try not to.'

Sara said: 'Mike! You can't!' Her voice shook. She blinked and looked from one to the other as though they were idiots.

Hannifin said: 'You'd better use *my* gun. The same gun that killed Kovarsky. The KGB is very thorough.'

Mike picked up the Beretta. 'In the living-room, Tim. If I shoot you out here you'll freeze to death.'

Hannifin nodded and moved into the house.

Sara pleaded: 'No, Mike, no! Please!'

Evans turned to her and said: 'Wait in the car.'

He went into the house. Hannifin was putting a log on the fire. He picked up a poker and stoked it.

Evans asked: 'When will they find you?'

'Before morning. Police patrols will find the Zil and report it to Krasnik, the local KGB chief. It's his car. He'll come screaming out here to find out what's happened. How are you travelling? As Michael Evans or Bentleigh Stringer?'

'Stringer. That's what my passport says.'

'Well, get going. I'll have to put out an alarm for Evans. You could be in danger.'

'How much do I tell Marakov?'

'Nothing. If he doesn't make it he could crack and talk. Tell him the Opel belongs to Sara.'

Evans nodded. He stood back half a dozen paces, pulled out the Beretta and shot Hannifin just in from the right armpit. Then he stepped swiftly forward, caught him and lowered him onto the floor.

He said: 'Good luck.'

He put back the Beretta and walked out of the building leaving the lights on.

He went to the car and found Sara sitting in the front seat. He opened the back door wide and went to Marakov. He squatted beside him.

'Marakov. Can you hear me?'

The Russian's lips moved. He said 'Yes' softly.

'Marakov. I'm going to try to move you into the car. Can you help yourself up?'

'I'll try.'

Evans pulled Marakov's arm upwards with his right hand and slid his left arm around his waist. Marakov was unsteady on his feet but they staggered drunkenly to the car. After a lot of effort and grunting Evans got him to lie on his side on the back seat. He shut the door.

As he opened the door to slide into the driver's seat, Sara got out of the car.

He asked: 'Where are you going?'

She hurried into the house without answering.

Evans saw her handbag on the seat. He opened it and found her lipstick. He pulled off the cap and eased out the lipstick from the small cylinder. He took the tiny roll of microfilm from his pocket, jammed it into the cylinder and put back the lipstick. Then he put the cap back on and put it back in the handbag. He wiped his fingers with his handkerchief and turned the ignition switch. He pressed the starter-button and the motor sprang to life with a deep healthy throb.

Sara came out of the house and got in beside him, her face stony.

After a few seconds she burst out: 'Why? Why?'

Evans said quietly: '*You* opted into this. Remember?'

He switched on the headlights, eased the front wheels past Kovarsky and swung toward the road.

20

Evans slowed the Opel down to pass a large van travelling in the opposite direction. The roads were covered with snow and occasional stretches of black ice, and without tyre-chains progress was slow. They had found the Opel without difficulty, safely hidden from the road among the trees. Before transferring Marakov to the Opel they made him stand up while Evans removed his coat and shirt, then tore the shirt into strips which Sara bandaged tightly round his chest, securing a folded handkerchief over the wound. Then they got him into the back of the Opel. Evans started the Opel's motor and left it running while he drove the Zil back to the side of the road, removed the key and threw it into the snow. Then he hurried back to the Opel and got in beside Sara. He drove it to the road and turned west. They had passed through the dark silent city of Wroklaw just before three o'clock.

Now Evans slowed down and pulled into the side of the road. He switched off the motor and left only the parking lights on. Sara had been sleeping, her head on his shoulder. She straightened as he switched on the interior light and leaned his arm over the seat to turn and look at Marakov.

'Are you losing any blood?'

'A little.'

'Do you feel all right?'

Marakov said softly: 'I am very happy.'

'Try a cigarette.' Evans turned to Sara. 'Light one for him.' She nodded and got a pack from her handbag. She twisted round onto her knees and put a cigarette between the Russian's lips. Then she found her lighter and lit it for him. He nodded and smiled his thanks. She turned to face the windscreen again and sat down. She put two cigarettes between her lips, lit them and passed one to Evans.

Evans wound down two of the windows a little to let the smoke out. He took a rag from the pocket in the door to wipe the condensation from inside the windows. Then he turned off the interior light and they sat smoking in the darkness for a time.

There was a long silence. Evans was thinking of their position and guessed they were not far from the town of Zagan, a few miles south of the Oder.

He said to Sara quietly: 'When we get to Zagan we split up. We'll drop you at the railway station. I want you to catch the first train to East Berlin.'

She blinked several times and saw the deadly serious look on his face.

He said earnestly: 'Collins. The time has come for you to do exactly as I say.'

She nodded. 'I promise.'

He leaned over and picked up the Crabb manuscript. He tore out the title page, crumpled it and threw it out of the window. Then he took out a ball-point pen and printed a new title on the fly-leaf. It read:

LOVE, HONOUR AND OBEY

A Novel by Sara Collins

He underlined the word *OBEY* and passed it to her.

'I want you to take this with you.'

She read it with some surprise, then smiled at him and put the manuscript on her lap.

He said: 'If anything happens to me I want you to ring Chauncey Bowes.' He wrote a telephone number on the bottom of page twenty.

She repeated the name. 'Chauncey Bowes.'

He nodded. 'He's in London. And give him the *message* I've put inside your lipstick.' When he saw her eyes jump he pointed backwards with his thumb toward Marakov. She nodded quickly.

Then he picked up the spool of film, opened the car door and threw it like a quoit into the snow-filled ditch off the side of the road. He closed the door and started the motor.

As they entered the outskirts of Zagan, she said: 'When will you cross?'

'I don't know.'

'Will you cross at Checkpoint Charlie?'

'I don't know.'

They drove into the dark sleeping town and pulled up a short distance from the old-fashioned railway station. He slid out and opened the car door for her. She climbed out carrying her handbag and the manuscript. He took her arm and led her several paces from the car and held her shoulders.

He said: 'When you get to East Berlin take a cab to Karl-Marx-Allee and change your appearance. Take off those spectacles and that fur coat and hat and buy yourself a drab-looking overcoat and some kind of hat. Buy a case to carry your fur coat. Then go into the Moskau restaurant. Have you got that?'

She nodded quickly.

He went on: 'Have lunch there. Take a long time over it. At three o'clock ring this number.' He took the manuscript from her and found page fifty and wrote a telephone number on it. 'When a man answers, simply say the word "sputnik" and tell him where you are. Then do whatever he says.' He gave her back the manuscript.

She nodded quickly, kissed him and hurried into the station. He watched her go. She was carrying Hannifin's microfilm, Marakov's manuscript and Karl's secret telephone number in East Berlin—their only hope of crossing the Wall.

He hoped to Christ she'd make it. He turned and got back into the car.

In the pale pre-dawn glow, two cars came slowly through the still white streets of Krakow. They turned off to the right at the Cloth Hall and went several blocks to a suburb of solid middle-class houses. They stopped before one of the best in the street. The first car was a police patrol car. The second, towed by a heavy rope, was a black Zil.

The front door of the Zil opened and a policeman slid out and closed the door. He untied the tow-rope from both cars and put it in the boot of the police car. Then he went to the front door of the house and rapped sharply with the heavy iron knocker.

There was a long wait in the early morning stillness. Then a porch light came on and the door opened. A compact pre-maturely bald man with a hard square sun-tanned face appeared. He was wearing striped flannel pyjamas and a thick brown dressing-gown. He glowered at the policemen.

'Yes?'

'Good morning, Comrade. I have a strange thing to report. We have just found your Zil. It was abandoned along the road to Katowice.'

The man looked stunned, jolted into instant wakefulness, and savage. 'What is this?' He looked with disbelief beyond the policeman at the two cars standing in front of his house. 'Where on the road to Katowice?'

'About a kilometre out of town. The key was gone, Comrade Krasnik! So we towed it here at once, thinking that——'

'Wait for me!' Krasnik snapped, and stepped back out of sight.

The policeman went down to the patrol car and stood by it, ready to get in.

After a short wait the door of the house slammed and Krasnik hurried to the Zil. He held up a key to them and said: 'Follow me, Comrades!'

140

He got into the car, started the motor after several tries, revved it up, then put it into gear and drove off at high speed. The police car followed, its back wheels spinning and its chassis yawing in the take-off.

The Zil streaked out along the road toward Wieliczka, turned off to the right along the road that led to the Vistula and slowed down to swing left into the drive that led to the farmhouse. The police car followed and swung in beside the Zil.

Krasnik was first out, his automatic drawn. Before him lay Kovarsky, stiff and frozen on the glistening flagstones. The lights in the house were still on, pale in the early morning glow. The two policemen sprang out, guns drawn, and surveyed the ghastly scene.

Krasnik led the way into the house. He stopped in the hall and saw the door standing wide open. They stepped across to it and looked into the dark cellar. In the light from the hallway they saw Boris, sprawled head first down the stone steps in a glutinous smudge of blood.

The KGB man uttered an oath and went into the living-room, the policemen following. They saw a third body.

Hannifin was lying face down on the floor, a wide pool of blood around his body and outstretched arm.

Krasnik quickly knelt beside him and rolled him over. Hannifin moaned. His handkerchief was red, held to his chest in a blood-streaked hand. His face was white. He opened his eyes and stared up at the Russian.

Krasnik asked: 'What happened, Comrade?'

Hannifin whispered hoarsely: 'Marakov—defecting. The Englishman——' He closed his eyes and swallowed.

Krasnik shook his shoulder. 'What Englishman?'

Hannifin's eyes opened again. 'Evans.'

Krasnik stood up. He turned to the policemen.

'Go and get an ambulance! We must get this man to hospital!'

'Yes, Comrade.'

The two men hurried out to the patrol car. A few seconds later it was speeding toward Krakow.

Krasnik did a quick search of the house, then strode back to the Zil, got in and followed the police car back to town. There were urgent things he had to do—urgent action to apprehend Marakov and Evans. He would have to go to his office and phone every border checkpoint between Bohumin to Kostrzyn—sixteen in all. Following this he would alert Arkov in East Berlin and Liebervich in Prague. Then he would phone General Zadikov, the Head of Department S in Moscow, and report details of his gruesome discovery and the prompt steps he'd taken to head off the murderers.

21

The train gave a long whistle and began to slacken speed. Some goods trucks, hauled by a straining engine, rumbled by. The silhouette of sheds slid by. With a sudden screech of couplings the train took the points and lurched away from the through-line. Two sets of rails formed black streaks in the snow outside the window as the train slowed to a jerking crawl. Finally, with a sigh of hydraulic brakes and a sudden flat blast of escaping steam, it ground to a halt. The station signs said GUBIN. It was the border.

Sara looked out of the window and saw a silent horde of peasants with bundles and battered cases and baskets waiting for Customs and Passport Control. There was a façade of dour buildings in smoke-stained stone and a long bleak expanse of platform, level with the ground. A few drab officials stood by, unshaven and unhappy-looking. No doubt they were cold and had been on shift all night.

'Passports! Customs!'

The conductor stepped into the carriage. A policeman came in behind him, and a plain-clothes man stood in the corridor. The conductor checked Sara's train ticket. Then the plain-clothes man stepped in and checked her passport and travel visas. Then the policeman asked in halting English to search her luggage. She handed him up her handbag. He looked around at the racks for her to indicate which case was hers. She pointed to her handbag, smiled, and said: 'Turysty.'

He took longer than necessary to look through her handbag

and gave it back to her. They processed the rest of the passengers in the carriage and left.

Sara hugged the manuscript under her fur coat and lit a cigarette. Across the platform she saw a sign over a door which said 'POLIZEI'. There was a grimy window beside it, lit from behind, a grey silhouette of a man's head and shoulders framed like a portrait. He was speaking on a telephone.

After a long delay doors clanged shut. The guard at the back of the train looked at his watch then held up his flag. The train started with a violent jerk and began to move through the cold drab scene with a series of explosive puffs. The nostalgic smell of coal-dust came in the windows as the train took the points and jerked harshly back onto the main line and accelerated with each passing second toward the snow-flaked countryside along the west bank of the Oder.

Five miles beyond Lubsko a train passed them. It whistled several times before it came to a level crossing. Evans guessed that Sara was in one of those dark carriages watching the car lights and wondering if they belonged to the Opel.

In the early light of dawn, the ramparts of Gubin came into view two or three kilometres ahead. He drew the car into the side of the road and braked. He switched off the motor and turned round to Marakov.

'Marakov.'

'Yes.'

Evans said: 'How did you expect to cross into West Berlin?'

'I have a Dutch passport—in the name of Kurt Van Hulssen.'

'Can you speak Dutch?'

'I have been learning Dutch and German.'

'What stamps does the passport have?'

'Helsinki, Moscow, Warsaw and Krakow—all the past few weeks. I am a Dutch tourist.'

'Do you also have an international driver's licence?'

'Yes.'

'What about your appearance?'

'The Van Hulssen has a picture taken when I was clean-shaven.'

There was a pause. Evans asked: 'As Marakov, would you be able to cross into East Germany without difficulty?'

'*East* Germany? Of course! I can travel anywhere this side of the Wall. I have a transit priority card issued by the KGB.'

'When you cross into East Germany will it be reported?'

'Yes. As a matter of course. Arkov insists on it. A border guard will ring him in East Berlin to report that I have passed into his territory.'

'Do you know Arkov?'

'I have had recent contact with him.'

'Will Arkov pass the information on to Moscow?'

'Not unless he has something to query.'

Evans thought for a few seconds. He looked at Marakov and said distinctly: 'You will cross into East Germany *alone*—as Marakov.'

Marakov looked up at him desperately. 'Must I?'

'It's the only way to give Van Hulssen a chance.'

The Russian shrugged. 'Whatever you say.'

'Will you be able to manage it? You'll have to drive.'

The Russian looked grim and in pain, but he nodded.

'Then we'd better change here. We're almost at the border.'

He climbed out and opened the back door and helped Marakov to sit up.

'Where is your KGB pass?'

Marakov's hand groped to his chest. Evans slipped a hand into the Russian's inside coat pocket. He drew out a leatherette holder and opened it. It held a parchment embossed document faced with plastic. He put it on top of the dashboard. Then he helped Marakov out of the car and made him stand up.

'Your passport and driver's licence. Marakov's.'

The Russian took them from his hip pocket and gave them to Evans, who put them with the pass. Evans took off his own gabardine overcoat and put it on the Russian and buttoned it up to the neck to hide the bloodstained bandages. Then he helped him into the car behind the wheel and shut the door. He went round the other side and got in beside him. He started the motor and let it idle.

Evans said: 'Drive to the border checkpoint and pass through, then find the road south to Cottbus and go out about a kilometre and stop. I will catch up with you.'

'Why Cottbus? Why south—away from Berlin?'

'Because Arkov will put a road-block between Gubin and Frankfurt.'

Marakov nodded. Evans told him to press down the clutch while he put the car in gear. Then he slid out, shut the door and stood back. Marakov eased out the clutch and the car moved off slowly toward Gubin.

Evans pulled his collar up and put his hands in his pockets and stood waiting in the half-light. About ten minutes later a dilapidated station-wagon rumbled into view, and Evans hailed the driver. The station-wagon slowed and Evans ran after it. As soon as it stopped he climbed in beside the driver, a bearded Pole. He uttered his grateful thanks in German and the driver simply nodded, eased out the clutch and drove toward the town.

At the border Evans produced his 'Bentleigh Stringer' passport and his Polish and East German transit visas. There was no hold-up.

As soon as they were out of sight of the guard-post, Evans thanked the Pole in German and got him to stop and got out. He walked through the town of Gubin and found the road that led south to Cottbus.

About a kilometre out of town he came upon the Opel. It was on the side of the road, its wheels pointing toward a deep ditch. Marakov had stopped it just in time. As he approached the car looked deserted. But when he drew level with it he found Marakov slumped across the front seat.

Evans forced him to move over a little so that he could jam himself in behind the wheel. He started the car and drove south-west, away from Gubin.

22

Within sight of the junction town of Cottbus, Evans slowed down. He swung right onto a narrow road that ran to the northern bank of the river Spree and pulled the car to a halt in a tree-dotted picnic ground.

He turned and said to Marakov: 'Anatoly, I'll have to leave you here awhile. This Opel's hot because it was driven across the border by Anatoly Marakov. It won't take Arkov long to get onto it. I'll walk into Cottbus and try to get another vehicle.'

The Russian nodded. His face was white and drawn. He looked beyond caring about his fate. Evans looked hard at him and wondered if he shouldn't take him to the nearest doctor and leave him. But he decided otherwise and closed the car door and walked into the pretty riverside town.

He found a used-car yard, but it was closed. While he filled in time waiting for the manager to arrive he went into a small café and had breakfast of what tasted like sawdust-filled sausages, with toast and coffee.

It was quite light now, though only a pale glow could be seen through the overcast in the east. He strolled around the town waiting for the shops to open. When they did he bought a safety razor, soap and a towel. Then he walked back to the used-car lot and waited.

Just before nine o'clock the manager arrived and unlocked the wire-mesh gates. He was a surly middle-aged man with stubbly black hair. Evans explained that his car had broken down five kilometres out along the road from the border crossing at Forst and that he wanted to buy a second-hand vehicle that would get him as far as Munich, where he would sell it. The German showed him a decrepit 1951 Skoda. After several tries he got the cold motor started. He took Evans for a ride around the block, and though it had a nasty whining sound and seemed to burn a lot of oil, it seemed reasonably roadworthy. Evans checked the tyres and bought it for the equivalent of one hundred pounds.

Then he drove it to a petrol station and filled up the tank and topped up the oil and water. He bought a package of sandwiches and a bottle of milk and drove back to the river bank.

He got a tin full of near-freezing water from the river and made Marakov sit up while he shaved him painfully with the safety razor. Then he helped him into the front seat of the Skoda, explaining that he'd probably have to take the wheel again before they reached East Berlin. While Marakov was eating the sandwiches, Evans drove the Opel in among some trees two hundred yards farther along and left it. He walked back to the Skoda and burnt all the documents connected with the identity of Anatoly Marakov.

He told the Russian: 'You are now Kurt Van Hulssen, for better or for worse.'

He slid into the Skoda and started the motor. They went through Cottbus onto the main road west, which gradually swung north towards Berlin.

Marakov seemed to be bearing up well, though he still looked pale and hollow-eyed. His freshly-shaven face had a naked look. The loss of his beard and moustache had considerably changed his appearance and his personality. Now he looked more apologetic than ever, more assailable. He looked young and insecure.

The Skoda ran well enough, but at Libbenau he checked the oil and found that the level was dangerously low. He had a quart put in and drove on toward Brand.

After a time he asked: 'Anatoly. When did you decide to defect?'

148

'Before I left Moscow. I had planned it for months.'

'Why?'

There was a long pause. Marakov said quietly: 'To answer that you'd have to know where and when I was born and how my father died. He was a writer in Moscow in the thirties. He objected to Stalin's purges and was among the millions who disappeared without trace. They arrested him one night and sent him to Siberia. We did not see him again.' After a brief pause he went on: 'My mother was left to raise six children. I was the eldest. She convinced us that my father had indulged himself in unrealities and dreams and brought us up as good Communists. It was the only answer to survival, she said. We must obey the State. Only then would we be allowed to live good lives.

'I had inherited some of my father's talent. I became a writer and translator. That was when Kovarsky was secretary of the Soviet Writers' Union. He gave me a job in the KGB's—in those days the MVD's—propaganda division. I was put in charge of translations of the foreign news sent in from the embassies. At this time I was attached to Smersh, Central Index. Several months ago a new department was formed——'

'Department S.'

He said in surprise: 'You knew about S? Yes. Department S. Kovarsky became its Chief of Operations, and he looked for writers who would work loyally for the State.' His tone had become bitter, self-mocking. 'I was on top of the list, and Kovarsky brought me into S. It soon became clear that my job was to plot against the underground writers.'

'How plot?'

'Become one of them. Win their confidence. Exchange confidences and writings. Talk about our desires, our plans to publish in the West. When I learned their innermost secrets I would tell Kovarsky, and one by one he would pounce on them. Sometimes there would be trials. But mostly they would just disappear. Then the persecution would continue. Their houses would be searched. Their wives would be badgered and questioned about their associations with other writers, and their children would be denied entry into universities and their whole future compromised.'

He smoked in silence for a time. 'Gradually, it sickened my soul. Gradually I thought my own thoughts and began to worship the real writers, even envy them. When I was a child I found a few lines my father had written—about thinking men in a reign of terror, how they withdrew into the forest, into the innermost secrecy of their beings. So inside my heart I became one of them. I came to know and love the more courageous of these men who were writing books and poems in the loneliness of their rooms in a sacred effort to keep awake the faculty of independent thought.

'I began to plan my escape. Kovarsky admired my ingenuity and had put me in a small section that originated projects. One day I remembered the Crabb *zapiska* that I'd originated in the days of Serov and the MVD. I decided here was my opportunity, for I had heard the legend of Korablov. They even sang the folk-song on television. So I wrote the first chapter and outlined the rest and submitted it to Kovarsky. He immediately saw in it a great chance to humiliate the British Secret Service. This had top priority because of Britain's success in publishing the works of Soviet underground and émigré writers. He was also after General Zadikov's job. He told me to go ahead and brought in a well known British defector to help me in relation to the SIS side.

'The biggest thing that had happened since Department S was formed was the defection of the British spy, Hannifin. He was one of several conquests of Doctor Eisendrath, a brilliant philosophy teacher at the University of Vienna. Hannifin had joined Department S and was given the task of working with Kovarsky to break the pipeline that took the works of Soviet underground writers to the West. I understand that they were effective in knocking out the Berlin operation.'

Evans said: 'You could say that.'

'But they wanted Stringer to go on operating for them, so

that they could use him. They opened up their own link with him—a loyal party member named Greta Ziegler. It was she who passed Part One of my manuscript to Stringer.'

'And the Korablov story?'

'All lies.'

Evans gave a tired resigned kind of chuckle. After a silence he asked:

'And the film?'

'A fake. The sound-track was made in London. A well-known television actor spoke the lines. He had no idea what it was for.'

'But Korablov exists?'

'Yes.'

'They've simply created the legend as fiction because he looks like Crabb?'

'Yes.'

'And Crabb? Your frogmen didn't see him?'

'Oh, they saw him all right. They were waiting for him. They knew all about him, had been shadowing him for days. Matthew Smith, of course.'

'Matthew Smith was real?'

'Yes. That part of it was true. Smith had told Strelchuk that Crabb was in an unfit condition to make the dive. Strelchuk was familiar with the type of breathing-apparatus Crabb was using. In his command he always insisted that divers equipped with it worked in pairs because it was dangerous below thirty-three feet, and any man wearing such a set at the limit of its safe depth stood a strong chance of contracting oxygen poisoning and losing his mouth-piece and drowning. Strelchuk's men were waiting for him. They saw him go under the cruiser, but before they could reach him he'd gone back to check his gear. Then he came back under the *Smotryashchi* and they saw him get into trouble and go down. That is all they know about Crabb.'

Evans was silent. A nagging question was on his mind. The missing head and hands. English experts had worked out that with the lungs full of water and with the weight of the leaden belt the body would have rested at a depth on or just above the sea-bed. They had worked out that the tides could have carried the body into Langston Harbour, where it could have been trapped by a wreck. The tide could have eventually torn it away—headless and handless?—and carried it on into Chichester Harbour.

Evans thought: I don't buy it. What had Krushchev meant when he'd referred to 'sharp moments' and 'certain underwater rocks'—if he hadn't meant a clash between frogmen with knives beneath the Russian ships? Or had Crabb been captured, questioned, then drowned, decapitated and his hands cut off under water and left to sink and drift? *Or had Marakov unwittingly stumbled on the truth?*

Marakov said: 'I am not very proud of myself.'

'What did you plan to do?'

'Use the manuscript to get a stake of money in the West, then defect in my own time. I planned the journey to Krakow as the first move.'

'What went wrong?'

'Kovarsky out-thought me. One day I got permission to search for some *zapiskas* in Central Index. The file I specifically asked to see was that of a writer named Markovich. It was only three from my own.'

'You mean there was a *zapiska* on *you*?'

'Yes. Kovarsky had me dead to rights. The file had me documented as an underground writer and an associate of other underground writers. It mentioned that my father was imprisoned for writing treasonable poems. It even listed the writers I had called on under instructions from himself!' After a brief pause he went on. 'I decided to make my move and applied for permission to go to Krakow because of my health. Kovarsky readily agreed. Then he gave me the name of Bentleigh Stringer, a London authors' agent who handled the works of the Soviet underground writers. He instructed me to contact Stringer through a girl named Greta Ziegler. I did this as soon as I arrived, sending the manuscript and full instructions to her through Arkov, the KGB man in East Berlin.'

'What about the ten thousand?'

'That was my own precondition, the way I hoped to outwit Kovarsky. But I hadn't realized that I was a pawn in a much larger game. I realize now that Kovarsky, with Hannifin's help, had planned your capture and enforced defection. By killing Danilov in front of Stringer's eyes they knew he would be too scared to venture behind the Iron Curtain. And knowing of your association with Stringer as an author, and the fact that you were an ex-SIS man, and in West Berlin, they knew that Stringer would plead with you to go to Krakow in his place.

'I knew nothing of this. I had planned to ask you to help me defect to the West. Then a message came out to me from Krasnik, the local KGB man, who loaned me the Zil, that Comrade Kovarsky would be arriving in Krakow in the morning and that I was to go to the airport and pick him up. Kovarsky horrified me by searching your room at the Dom Turysty. And even then, since your room was booked in the name of Stringer, I still did not know you were Michael Evans. And then we——'

'Hold it. Sit up!'

A police siren sounded behind them. A patrol car drew level and waved to Evans to pull in to the side of the road. Evans braked gradually and stopped. The police car swung in front of them and stopped.

Two Volks-Polizei sprang out and walked back on each side of the Skoda. Evans and Marakov produced their 'Stringer' and 'Van Hulssen' drivers' licences. Then they were asked for their passports. After examining them and asking several questions, they turned their attention to the Russian and asked if he was ill. Marakov told them he had a bad tooth-ache and Evans said he was driving his friend to a dentist in West Berlin.

The Polizei let them proceed.

23

Commissar Vsevolod Arkov looked up at the huge wall-map of Germany and focused his eyes on the portion which showed the road between Cottbus and Wusterhausen. In a few minutes he would have them. No one could get through the net he'd set to catch Marakov and Evans.

Arkov had been on the job since early morning, when the border guard at Gubin had phoned him at his home to report that KGB operative Marakov had crossed the border into East Germany. Of course, the name had registered at once. Marakov was the member of Smersh, Department S, whom Arkov had put in touch with Greta Ziegler a fortnight ago. He and Marakov had exchanged correspondence and telephone calls. When Arkov received the early morning call from the border guard, he'd thought it quite natural that Marakov should now be coming to East Berlin to consult with him. No doubt he wanted Arkov to arrange a meeting with Fräulein Ziegler.

But then, only a few minutes later, had come the call from Comrade Krasnik in Krakow, giving him the gruesome details of his early morning discovery out at the farmhouse.

Arkov's immediate move had been to set up a road-block between Gubin and Frankfurt and another between Frankfurt and Erkner. Then he had put a patrol on the road between Gubin and Cottbus.

As soon as he reached his office he rang the Gubin guard-post and obtained a list of all transients who had passed across the border since midnight. One of them, he learned, was named Bentleigh Stringer. Arkov immediately remembered that this was the name of the English literary agent Marakov had directed Greta Ziegler to contact in West Berlin.

Soon after nine he rang Fräulein Ziegler at her office and learned that Herr Stringer had gone to Krakow to pick up the Korablov manuscript from Marakov.

Like a blood-hound on the scent he rang Krasnik and asked whether there had been two Englishmen concerned—Evans *and* Stringer. Krasnik had never heard of Stringer. He said he would ask Comrade Hannifin the moment he regained consciousness after the operation.

The police patrol on the Gubin–Cottbus road reported the finding of the Opel on the eastern bank of the Spree within walking distance of Cottbus.

Arkov ordered the patrol to check on all trains out of Cottbus and make inquiries at the local State-controlled used-car depot and find out if anyone had bought a car that morning.

Within minutes the Polizei officer rang through the information that a Skoda had been sold to an English tourist. His name: Bentleigh Stringer.

Arkov quickly recalled that Marakov had crossed the border at Gubin *alone* in the Opel. The Opel had been abandoned, and a Skoda had been purchased—by Stringer.

This proved beyond doubt that Marakov and Stringer were travelling together.

And in Arkov's mind Stringer was Evans.

He now put a road-block a few kilometres south of Wusterhausen and had one of his monitors make radio contact with police patrols operating north-west of Cottbus.

One of them had already reported sighting the Skoda heading north on the East Berlin highway just out of Brand.

Arkov's hands were clenched together and he rubbed his palms slightly. His eyes were still riveted on the wall-map—on the road just south of Wusterhausen. Within minutes the Skoda would arrive at the road-block. It would then be the triumphant moment he'd been waiting for—when he would ring General Zadikov and report the capture of Marakov and Evans.

A sudden memory clouded the prospect. He thought of the recent defection of another Department S man, Rodya Vishniak, and of General Zadikov's vituperative criticism. Certainly, Arkov's subsequent liquidation of Danilov, Walkley and Schmidt may have partly rehabilitated him in the eyes of the General, but he could not afford another defection from his area—certainly not of another Department S man.

Arkov turned to look across at the other wall-map which showed every street and lane in Berlin, on both sides of the Wall. He followed the line of the wall for a few moments. It was *his* wall and he had every confidence in it. It had done the job it had been put there for. His eyes followed it along Bismarckstrasse, cut off at Unter-den-Linden, crossed Potsdamer Platz, and blocked off Stresemannstrasse and Friedrichstrasse. He looked along the cleared strip East of the Wall, where buildings had been dynamited and cleared and others had been condemned, sealed and cordoned off. Between these and the Wall was the 'shoot-on-sight' area, and he visualized the towers, look-outs, search-lights, guard-posts, patrol cars and police covering it. Yet somewhere along here Rodya Vishniak had crossed the Wall, with the help of the underground. It was infuriating that such a thing could still happen. His special force had already destroyed scores of tunnels and other means of crossing to West Berlin. His soldiers had slaughtered hundreds of would-be defectors since the Wall was built. Yet there were still people stupid enough and traitorous enough to try it.

Vishniak, he thought, had caught him off-guard. That could never happen again.

A uniformed orderly brought him a tray of coffee and toast and he sat down at his desk to enjoy it, swivelling round so that he could look every now and then at the section of the wall-map showing the road-block south of Wusterhausen.

24

Snow was falling steadily as the drab buildings of East Berlin glided past the carriage windows. There were several stops as the train neared the East Berlin Bahnhof. After a time the train took the points with a screech of couplings and rattled across the tracks of a dozen cross-lines, then swung in parallel to them and gradually slowed to a crawl. Finally it came to a jarring halt.

Sara rose with the other passengers, pushing the manuscript securely under her left arm beneath the fur coat. She went along the narrow corridor in a slow-moving queue of people and came to the end of the carriage.

A conductor was helping the passengers down the long drop to the concrete platform, which was at ground level. Two uni-formed Polizei stood scrutinizing the passengers as they left the train.

Sara reached the top step and looked about her. She clutched the fur coat around her and held her handbag securely in her right hand. The conductor reached up and held her left arm. As she stepped down she felt the manuscript slip from under her elbow. It fell with a *slap* onto the concrete.

Before she could reach the ground, the older of the two Polizei stooped and picked up the manuscript. He opened the cover and read the title page. He translated for the benefit of his colleague and the conductor, then graciously handed it to Sara.

'*Schreiben Sie Bücher?*'

She stood blinking up at him, then smiled and nodded. They laughed.

She turned and hurried along the platform to the wide Bahnhof entrance and went out to the pavement. A cab moved up from the rank and she climbed in and asked the driver to take her to Karl-Marx-Allee.

When they reached Brand, Evans really knew what he'd bought in the Skoda. It took nearly another quart of oil. They went on. Within a few kilometres of Wusterhausen, on the outskirts of East Berlin, Evans pulled the car in to the side of the road.

'What is wrong?' Marakov asked.

'There'll be several road-blocks between here and Karl-Marx-Allee. You must go on alone.'

'But why?'

'Because they don't know your second identity yet, but they know mine. And two of us together would be a give-away. We will have to make it alone.'

'What will *you* do?'

'Go on foot. Get a bus somewhere.'

Marakov agreed reluctantly. Evans opened the door and slid out into the falling snow. He leaned in and helped Marakov to move behind the wheel.

Evans said: 'Once you're into the suburbs, dump the car and catch a cab through Checkpoint Charlie. Go to the Europa Hotel.' The Russian nodded. His face was ashen, his mouth drawn. 'Hang on, Anatoly. You'll have a doctor in under an hour.'

Evans shut the door and stepped back. The Skoda rumbled off toward Wusterhausen. He turned and left the road and trudged across a snow-covered field east of the road.

The Skoda began to make a knocking noise. It quickly got worse, and the windscreen wipers struggled and scraped against the falling snow. Marakov felt the loss of power. He trod on the accelerator, but though the engine roared there was no pull, only a louder knocking. He changed down, but there was no improvement. The noise became worse and the car slowed to a crawl. Then, with a loud metallic bang, it stopped altogether. The engine had seized. He sat behind the wheel wondering what to do.

After a time he got out painfully and closed the door. He stood leaning against the vehicle. The snow was falling in solid flakes. He didn't know how long he would be able to stay on his feet. He struggled along and half sat on the front mudguard, his hands behind him to take some of the weight, and leaned forward to relieve the pain in his bleeding wound.

A battered utility van came along and Marakov lifted one arm. The driver braked and pulled in in front of the Skoda. Marakov staggered to it and told the driver that his car had broken down. The German driver opened the door and let him into the front seat. The van started forward up the long rise. As they reached the crest, Marakov saw a road-block about two hundred yards ahead. The van joined the queue of vehicles waiting to go through.

In less than five minutes they were past the road-block and entering the outskirts of the East Berlin suburb of Wusterhausen.

Commissar Arkov was shaken.

The Skoda had been found broken down not two kilometres from Wusterhausen, and somehow Marakov and Evans had got past the road-block!

Immediately the pattern of the search changed. Now Arkov concentrated on a thorough scrutiny of every citizen abroad in the streets of East Berlin. He rang Greta Ziegler and obtained a description of Stringer. He rang Moscow and asked Smersh to radio a picture of Anatoly Marakov.

To double-check, he rang the Dom Turysty and asked the receptionist for a description of the man who had booked in as Bentleigh Stringer. The description of him—'medium height, compact, dark-haired'—was nothing like Greta Ziegler's description of Stringer—'large, floridly handsome, puffed up like a bullfrog'. The man Arkov was looking for was Evans.

And another fact came from the call to the Dom Turysty. The Englishman had been seen a lot with an American girl named Sara Collins—small, pretty, wearing a short fur coat, fur hat, and large spectacles.

Then Krasnik rang from Krakow to tell him that Hannifin had become conscious after the operation and had told him that Evans had come to Krakow in place of Stringer.

As Krasnik had met Marakov he was able to give Arkov a description—'tall, slim, stooped shoulders, bespectacled, brown beard'.

Arkov phoned the three descriptions to Polizei headquarters and ordered a full-scale search using every possible man.

Now he sat at his desk and nibbled at a few sandwiches and drank coffee and stared at the wall-map of Berlin. How? How could it have happened? Nobody resembling any of those descriptions had passed through the road-block near Wusterhausen.

He took action to extend the search to rail and bus transport and put through another call to Moscow. He asked Smersh to find out if there was a picture in its files of Marakov, taken *without* his beard, and to radio any such picture urgently.

Presently one of the monitors reported that a girl answering to the description of Sara Collins had already arrived in East Berlin on the train from Krakow.

Another monitor reported that none of the three had so far attempted to cross through Checkpoint Charlie.

Evans had entered the outskirts of the metropolis at a point he judged to be midway between Wusterhausen and Königs. He followed a street that led through a drab mass-built housing area and came to a market square. He went into a store and bought a plastic raincoat.

Then he came out and stood at a bus-stop with a group of people. After a time a bus came along and he boarded it. It was already crowded and he had to stand.

The utility van went all the way to Unter-den-Linden. Marakov thanked the driver and got out.

He stood with his back against a lamp post and waited for a taxi. When one came he waved and it swung in. He struggled into the back seat and asked the driver to take him to West Berlin.

As the car went toward the checkpoint Marakov leaned back across the seat, almost lying down. He was exhausted and in great pain. The driver caught sight of him in the rear-vision mirror and said:

'Are you ill, Comrade?'

Marakov nodded.

Evans got off the bus in Karl-Marx-Allee. He found a telephone booth and went in and dialled a number.

A male voice answered.

'Blenheim.'

Evans said in German: 'Are you still as quick as a sputnik?'

The voice said: 'Quicker. What is it you want done?'

'A moving job this afternoon.'

He hung up. Anyone overhearing the call would have heard the man say 'Hallo!' several times before hanging up in disgust.

Evans went into the Moskau restaurant.

He saw Sara sitting alone. She wore a cute hat and a grey raincoat. Her mouth dropped open and relief swept her face as she caught sight of him. Then she put her head down and picked up her coffee cup.

He chose a table several yards away and sat down. When the waitress came up he ordered chicken à la Kiev.

It was just ten past three when Karl entered the restaurant. He was a tall fair man with a slightly humorous lantern-jawed face. His keen blue eyes seemed to sweep across the scene without seeing anyone. He hesitated, then went through to the toilet.

Evans waited for him to come out then rose and went to

Sara's table. He smiled and leaned across at her and said in a low voice:

'Don't look. Follow the man who has just come out of the toilet. He will have a vehicle outside. Get into it. Give me the brush-off and walk out.'

She was blinking up at him.

He said firmly: 'Give me the brush-off—*now*! Get going!'

She said: 'Get lost!'

She rose haughtily and walked from the restaurant. He watched her pick up the case she'd cloaked at the hat-check counter and go on through to Karl-Marx-Allee.

Evans went back to his table, lit a cigarette and finished his coffee. Then he paid his bill and walked out under the critical eye of the cashier.

When he stepped out onto the pavement in Karl-Marx-Allee he saw Karl getting into a blue-grey Fiat van. He walked leisurely down to the van and slid into the front seat beside Karl, the driver.

'Hallo, Karl.'

'Mike.'

The two men shook hands quickly. Karl started the motor. Evans twisted round and saw Sara sitting shivering in the back of the van. He said: 'Hallo, Collins,' and introduced her to Karl. Karl released the brake and moved off, easing out into the traffic. Two blocks along he turned off the Allee toward the Wall. They went about a hundred yards from the boulevard and pulled into the kerb in front of the people's market. Karl switched off the motor.

'I have a stall here,' he explained. 'I use temporary assistants. The guards are used to me.'

He stepped out and opened the back of the van and helped Sara down. She was carrying her case. Evans took it from her, opened it, took out the manuscript and rolled it up in his hand and put the case back into the van.

'My fur!' she protested.

Evans shook his head. 'No luggage.'

Karl handed them a crate each to carry in. They entered the market and walked single file through the crowds of shoppers to a wire-mesh stall at the end of the building. Karl unlocked the padlock. They stooped to go under the counter and entered a tiny storage room and set down their crates. Karl immediately closed the door and switched on the light. He lifted the lid of a large wooden box filled with cabbages and proceeded to take them out and put them on a table. When he'd emptied it he said:

'Go down and wait for me. I have a stall to run till five.'

Evans nodded. He slipped the manuscript into the front of his shirt, buttoned it up and stepped into the box, avoiding the trap-door. He pulled up the lid and stepped through. He found a steel ladder going straight down into blackness. Karl lifted Sara into the box. She followed Evans down.

The long line of vehicles was stacking up beyond the Eastern checkpoint. It was snowing steadily and the distant buildings of East Berlin looked stark against the pale grey sky. The usual knot of people stood and watched the vehicles coming through. The same expressions on different faces. They stood silently and waited.

The major joined the M.P. at the observation window and peered through at the ever-lengthening queue. He lit a cigarette and got his binoculars.

The M.P. was droning his commentary: 'Fiat halted at first control. Driver escorted to Vopo hut.' He turned to the major. 'There's sure lots of activity across there this afternoon. There's another official car just arriving.'

The major trained his binoculars on the opposite checkpoint. 'That's what I was thinking. Seems to be a lot of chin-wag.'

After a time he went out of the hut and spoke to one of the guards standing behind the wall of sandbags. The guard nodded. The major came back to the door of the hut.

The queue made snail-like progress. Vopos on motorcycles patrolled up and down both lanes. There was a tense atmosphere as the Polizei sullenly went about their work and deliberately slowed down the procedure. After five minutes the queue moved forward the length of one vehicle.

The time dragged by and the sky grew darker. The arc-lights came on, covering the East and West checkpoints and the stretch of No Man's Land between them and bathing the whole scene in an unnatural glow.

Marakov's taxi was in the queue. In front was a green DKW. They had been stationary for five minutes. Marakov lay back against the hard upholstery, fighting pain, fighting nausea and tiredness. No longer was he fighting fear. That had gone a long time ago. Now he closed his eyes and thought of the long tenuous trail from Moscow. If he'd stayed there his future would have been certain. At any moment his *zapiska* would come out and he would snugly disappear and never be heard of again. There'd be no trial. Like his father he would be sent away—to withdraw into the forest, into the innermost secrecy of his being.

Ahead of him the counter-balance dropped. The barrier pivoted up. A Mercedes was waved through. The queue moved forward one more place.

25

At five o'clock an alarm bell sounded, three sharp rings. It was the signal for the shoppers hurriedly to complete their purchases and vacate the market. Below the stall in the blackness Evans and Sara heard the shuffle of footsteps. As time went by the noise gradually diminished, and after a long time there was comparative silence.

Sara said: 'Is Marakov coming with us?'

'No.'

'Where is he?'

'We had to split up,' Evans said shortly.

They remained silent. He thought of Marakov and hoped he'd got through. Evans couldn't have chanced making Karl responsible for a wounded man—particularly a member of the KGB. He'd even thought of the possibility that Marakov's defection was a trap, laid by Zadikov and Arkov, triggered by Vishniak's recent defection. No. He couldn't have taken the chance.

A soft clatter sounded above their heads. The trap-door swung up and a pale shaft of light came through. And presently a man's feet and legs reached down and contacted the rungs of the ladder. It was Karl and he held a torch. He came down and handed the torch to Evans, then went up again. He gently lowered the trap-door, leaving room for only his wrist. He put his hand through and dislodged a board that was holding the cabbages piled against the wall of the box. They came tumbling over the trap-door as he pulled his hand out and let it down. He came down to them and got Evans to direct the beam of the flashlight onto the concrete floor along the wall. He stooped and picked up an iron bar. He carried this up the ladder and jammed it through a metal loop screwed onto the bottom of the trap-door. He came down the ladder again and whispered:

'Follow me.'

He took the torch from Evans and moved silently through the darkness. They followed him through the basement of a huge warehouse below the market building. It was piled with packing cases which had been stacked to leave a narrow corridor.

At the end he moved one of the cases from beside the wall. There was a man-hole in the concrete floor. He gave Evans the flashlight and told him to go first. Evans lowered himself through and found another steel ladder. He went down it and Sara followed. Then Karl came through, put the iron disc in place over the man-hole and came down. They were standing on a large timber loading pallet. There was a square room with a concrete floor covered in two inches of water. There was a hole in the opposite wall that looked as if it had been gouged out with a crowbar.

Karl said: 'It's safe to talk here, so I'd better give you the score.' His north-country English accent came as a shock to Sara. 'You're about to go under the Wall. It's not at all safe. We haven't been able to tunnel all the way. We take this tunnel here, which doesn't lead us very far. We have to go through some condemned apartment buildings that have been sealed off just this side of No Man's Land. Then there's an open yard that they run testing instruments over every other day, so we can't tunnel under it. Then there's a barrier-wall at the end of the yard, and then No Man's Land, which we go under. Okay?'

Evans nodded. 'We're in *your* hands.'

Karl moved across the waterlogged floor to the opening. Evans picked Sara up and slung her over his shoulder. His shoes squelched in the ice-cold water. He put her down in the mouth of the tunnel, through which planks had been placed on building bricks above water level. They went on more than a hundred yards through an ancient drainage system. Karl's torch-beam lit the way through the blackness. Occasionally a pair of small eyes flashed ahead and a rat scampered through the tunnel. At the end of it there was a solid face of blackened stone. A ladder led up from it.

Karl waited for them here and said: 'This leads up into the condemned buildings on the edge of No Man's Land. There are continuous patrols through the whole area.'

He led the way up the ladder. They found themselves in a large bare room with grimy broken windows covered on the outside with heavy wire mesh. Light from nearby searchlights filtered into the room. Karl led them to the wall the windows were in.

Footsteps grated on the covered drive outside.

They flattened against the wall as a torch-beam flashed at one of the windows and swept the room. After a time the light went off and the footsteps came to the next window and the beam searched the room. Then the light went out and the footsteps scrunched out of earshot.

They went on, room by room, through the derelict building. At the end they came to a door.

Karl whispered: 'This stretch is the dangerous one. There's a searchlight on a tower sweeping the area and there are guards on towers and roof-tops who shoot at anything that moves. You have to move fast as soon as the light sweeps through.'

He opened the door a crack. A few seconds later blinding white light flooded the yard before them. Then it was gone.

Karl counted nine seconds.

The searchlight swept through again.

He opened the door, slid through, closed it and was gone. Through the narrow opening, Evans and Sara watched him race across the long flat yard, veer to the right and flatten himself against the wall in a narrow strip of shadow.

The searchlight swept through. Evans opened the door and

shoved Sara through. He watched her run full tilt across the yard and join Karl in the shadow.

Evans waited. The light flooded in and was gone. He opened the door, slipped through, closed it and ran. He reached the shadow and collided sharply with Sara. She was jolted sideways and, in the shock, dropped her handbag. It fell onto the concrete, open. Its contents spilled out.

'My lipstick!' she gasped.

They watched the gold lipstick holder roll across the concrete and come to a halt in a drain in the centre of the yard.

Karl hissed: 'Never mind your bloody lipstick!'

Evans whispered: 'There's a microfilm in it. Hold it, Karl. I'll get it.'

'Wait!'

Karl squatted in the corner. He ran his fingers round one of the large stones at the base of the wall. Suddenly the false front of the stone came away in his hands, revealing a black space. He told Sara to go down, backwards, feet first. She slid through into cavernous blackness. Then Karl followed.

Evans waited, flattened against the wall.

The searchlight swept the yard. The shiny gold cylinder glinted in the flood of light.

The searchlight swung back sharply to the spot. The yard was bathed in light as bright as day. The tiny holder shone like a diamond.

Now the beam moved manually and searched the yard. Evans moved to the corner and flattened himself against the stone-work. The light cut down to a sharp line inches in front of his shoes.

He stood still and waited.

Presently, the light moved off and swung into its normal nine-second sweep. Evans waited for it to pass twice, then ran. He raced forward, crouching low, and pounced on the lipstick. As he turned to come back the light swung sharply back to him, catching him in the centre of its beam.

A German voice cut through the night and a siren blasted with an urgent clamour of sound.

He raced back through the blinding glare as a machine-gun opened up from a nearby tower. As he flung himself into the shadow and crawled head first through the cavity a scorching pain seared into the back of his thigh.

As he went down the ladder hand over hand into the blackness, other machine-guns opened up above, and other sirens rent the air. Bullets ripped into the yard with a loud clatter of sound. Another searchlight was trained onto the spot and sirens screamed as cars swarmed into the area.

Karl caught his shoulders, lowered him down and pulled him to his feet.

'Come on!'

He turned along the narrow tunnel, his torch flashing ahead. Sara followed, then Evans. They had to crouch because the tunnel was low. They went along for fifty yards or more.

A voice sounded behind them, orders barked in the yard. Then they heard someone coming down the ladder.

Karl stopped and turned, shining his torch into a cavity on the left. He pushed Sara through, then Evans, and slid in after them after extinguishing the flashlight.

There was a silence, then voices, and a beam of light came through the tunnel, wavered, grew brighter.

Evans lay on the ground and drew his Beretta. He wriggled to the corner and fired upwards, aiming just below the torchlight. There was a scream and a clatter. The torch fell to the ground, its beam facing away. Its beam caught a German soldier. He was crouching as he came along the tunnel toward them, tommy-gun held tensely before him. Evans fired. The German stiffened and fell on his face. There was another soldier immediately behind. Evans shot him. The torch-beam showed the ghostly figure of another soldier on the ladder. Evans shot him in the back and he fell to the ground. Evans sent two more shots at the mouth of the tunnel, then turned and shouted:

'Go! Go now!'

Karl took Sara's arm and hurried through the tunnel, his torch shining ahead. Evans picked up the German's flashlight and held it on the ladder as he backed up the tunnel. At the sight of a leg venturing onto the rungs he fired.

After a few more yards the tunnel curved and put him out of the line of fire. He turned and hurried after Karl and Sara, his flashlight searching ahead.

'Hurry!' Karl hissed, and he limped forward, crouching low.

He saw them ahead now. He came up to them. He saw Karl reach up and pull down a switch. He heard a sliding sound then a bang behind him. He turned and saw that a steel door had slid down, blocking the tunnel. Behind it came the muffled roar of machine-gun fire and the clatter of bullets rattling against the steel plate on the far side of the earth-filled panel that formed the barrier.

Karl stretched up and pulled another switch.

A muffled blast shook the earth around them and the steel door shook in its mountings. The tunnel on the Eastern side had been collapsed with dynamite.

Several minutes later they reached a street lamp on Blucher-strasse.

Karl said abruptly: 'I leave you here.'

Evans looked at him questioningly. He knew better than to ask him why. He said: 'Sorry about your tunnel.'

Karl grinned and shrugged. 'Tunnels are expendable.'

'C will be upset.'

Karl shrugged. 'A tunnel is an idea, an unstoppable urge. There'll always be a tunnel.'

Evans nodded.

A taxi came along and Karl hailed it. When it stopped he helped Evans and Sara into it.

Evans told the driver to take them to the checkpoint.

26

The M.P. at the observation window said: 'Green DKW all clear. Coming through to second checkpoint.'

The barrier was raised and the DKW crossed to the Western checkpoint. A brown-and-white taxi was next in line. Two Vopos stood by. One of them opened the door of the taxi and a man climbed out. He was wearing a gabardine raincoat. Under escort, he walked unsteadily into the hut.

After a few seconds a taxi came along the Western side of the Wall and stopped. The back door opened and Sara got out. She helped Evans out. He had a handkerchief tied round his left thigh. She paid the taxi and helped him as he walked to the checkpoint hut.

They saw the man in the gabardine overcoat come out of the Vopo hut. He was holding his forearm across his stomach and he walked with difficulty, his shoulders hunched. Sara's hand tensed on Evans's arm when she saw him. She recognized Marakov without his beard. They watched him lurch to the taxi and climb in, the door close after him.

The M.P. said: 'Taxi cleared. One passenger. All clear to cross.'

The counter-balance dropped. The barrier swung up. The taxi came slowly onto No Man's Land.

Sara blinked several times and moistened her lips. Evans was checking the distance. Seventy yards, sixty yards, fifty . . .

'Halt das Taxi!' a voice rang out.

A Volks-Polizei officer had come from the hut.

The German sentry midway between the checkpoints stepped out in front of the cab. His sub-machine-gun was tilted at the driver.

The car brakes squealed. The tyres skidded on the bitumen. The car halted.

The officer and two Vopos strutted to the taxi.

The officer said to Marakov:

'Where did you stay in Krakow?'

Marakov looked at him blankly. He said: 'With friends.'

'What is their name?'

'The Cherniaks. Their daughter lives in Amsterdam.' Marakov swayed. He had difficulty in speaking. He had to hang on to the bar behind the front seat to stop from collapsing.

'What is the matter, Comrade? You are sick?'

Marakov nodded. 'My—appendix perhaps. I will see a doctor as soon as I cross the Wall.'

The Vopo officer looked hard at the drawn white face. He stepped back and slammed the door shut. The guard stepped aside.

The driver muttered something below his breath, released the brake and eased out the clutch. The taxi moved forward.

Evans watched the distance. Fifty yards, forty yards . . .

A car siren screamed into earshot.

Thirty yards . . .

An official Zil of the Soviet administration came swarming up the outside lane and skidded to a stop before the Eastern checkpoint. The back door opened and a man sprang out.

Twenty yards . . .

'Arkov,' Evans whispered.

Arkov was holding a black folder. He opened it and pointed to the picture it held—as three Vopo officers gathered round him.

One of them turned instantly and pointed toward the taxi. He said something quickly to Arkov.

Arkov screamed:

'Halt das Taxi!'

The guard on No Man's Land swung about and sent a single shot over the hood of the taxi.

The driver swore and braked.

Ten yards to go . . .

'Go on!' Marakov hissed. 'Go on!'

The driver turned with a hopeless look and lifted his hands with a shrug.

Marakov opened the door and stumbled out. Leaning forward almost double he pulled himself along the car and lurched onto the road, his legs wobbling under him.

'*Schiess' jenen Mann!*' Arkov shouted.

Five yards to go . . .

Marakov staggered forward in the glaring white light from the arcs. His movements were like slow-motion. He tried to hurry but everything about him was heavy and impeding, as though he were immersed in milky water at the bottom of the sea.

He dimly saw two figures far ahead. One was Evans, the other the American girl. They were screaming something at him.

He heard the shots behind him and felt them strike his body like hot skewers of steel as his legs kept running under him and his body sprawled forward. He felt himself sinking and saw a headless man floating ahead of him in the gloom as the darkness closed in.

The M.P.s leapt forward and dragged him across the line. They rolled him over to examine him. He was already dead. Evans turned and moved away. Sara, holding his arm, walked with him to the taxi.

27

Cookie brought in the tea tray and departed silently.

C and Chauncey Bowes watched Evans as he completed turning the pages of the bulky dossier—the enlarged contents of the microfilm.

Evans turned the last page and nodded. 'Maybe it's worth our losses.' He was thinking principally of Walkley. He put a lump of sugar in his tea and stirred it. Then he looked from Bowes to Control. 'You knew about Department S *before* Vishniak's defection.'

Neither man answered. They sipped their tea in silence.

Evans said: 'My recruit, Hannifin, discovered S in Vienna and flew to London to report it to you. He went over my head.'

C looked guilty. 'Don't blame Hannifin, Mike. That's how he was briefed.'

'I see.' Evans's tone was terse. Chauncey shifted uncomfortably in his chair and wouldn't look at him.

C said softly: 'We knew about Department S even before Hannifin but we didn't know its name. We've known for some time that Soviet writers were being forced to work for Smersh, both to apprehend underground writers and to attack the West. When Hannifin's worth became apparent we decided he was the man for Moscow. And we decided you'd both work better if *you* didn't know that Hannifin was about to stage a defection. We didn't want to prejudice the Vienna operation or put the Czech underground in any danger.'

'Who warned Pravja about Hannifin's possible double-game?'

'We did. But he didn't know that.'

Evans sipped his tea. It tasted sour. He would have liked to have stood up and poured it over Chauncey Bowes's obscene pink scalp. He asked: 'Was Eisendrath suspected before Tim spotted him for what he was?'

C said: 'Yes. Chauncey tumbled to him. He'd been watching teachers of philosophy, psychology, social studies, history, economics and so on. As Hannifin's dossier plainly states, Russia is frightened at the ground she has lost to Red China with the youth of the world through Mao's philosophy. She is spending millions in a campaign to convert Western teachers to teach one total-philosophy that will save the world from the Mao Revolution.'

Chauncey put in intensely: 'They're making gains in the West, by simply teaching that Democracy has no future and blaming the disorder of anarchy on Mao!'

C nodded, tapping the dossier. 'This tells us what they're doing throughout America and Britain and the rest of the Western world, how they're putting into the hands of all the splinter groups a blue-print for defying law and order, and showing them how a small flame can soon become a raging bushfire. The intelligentsia are telling the mixed-up students that democracy is finished and that anarchy is a democracy-founded disease, and that what is needed in the world of tomorrow is an idealistic total-philosophy.'

Evans asked: 'What are you doing about it?'

C passed the ball to Chauncey, who said: 'We're getting into the fight to teach youth the value of freedom of thought —above pot, protest, or the pop-tune of the moment. Propaganda in the mass-media has taken possession of the unthinking, defenceless souls, utilizing interests and influences without regard to right or wrong.' He pounded the table gently. '*Truth* itself has got to take the shape of propaganda in order to reach the ears and eyes of men. But—and it's a very important but—freedom of thought can only be retained by mastery of ourselves. All activity of the mind is tied up with the responsibility for the freedom of mankind. So we must never have the arrogant censorship of a State-power that selects and forbids!'

Evans was stroking his chin. C felt that theoretical discussion bored him. Evans could see it, of course. Sinyavsky. Daniel. Solzhenitsyn. But he was trying to strike a mental balance between Chauncey's high-flown sentiments and the violence of the last few weeks.

C tapped the dossier and said abruptly: 'A copy of this has been sent to the President of the United States through the CIA.'

Evans nodded. 'And what about Hannifin?'

C and Bowes exchanged a glance and smiled. C said: 'He's been promoted. Taken Kovarsky's job. He's now Chief of Operations of Department S.'

Evans couldn't resist it. 'Not bad for an Evans recruit.'

'An Evans recruit,' C conceded, but Evans wasn't sure that even this was true.

'Arkov?'

'Fired in disgrace. Zadikov saw to that. I believe he's in Vladivostok.' He added sternly: 'By the way, I was most upset about Karl's tunnel.'

'And the Crabb manuscript?'

'A red herring. It mixes fact and fiction dangerously. The public wouldn't know which was which. Since the author confessed to you that it was all lies, we've confiscated it. Brayne-Watts have cancelled their bank-draft, with our help. And Stringer has been reimbursed, so your thousand's safe.'

'It's safe all right. It's been spent on a fur coat.'